Stranger from Berlin

Beverley Hemsford

Also by the Author

Julie
A captivating novel with many twists and turns

With Rucksack and Bus Pass
Walking the Thames Path

Roots in Three Counties
Family history research

A Touch of Autumn Gold
A light-hearted insight into the older generation
and how they deal with life

The Golden Anklet
A love story set against family secrets and intrigue

Path of Injustice
The experiences of a young girl in the 18th century

Stranger

from

Berlin

BEVERLEY HANSFORD

Matador
9 Priory Business Park,
Wistow Road, Kibworth Beauchamp,
Leicestershire. LE8 0RX
Tel: 0116 279 2299
Email: books@troubador.co.uk
Web: www.troubador.co.uk/matador
Twitter: @matadorbooks

Edited by Helen Banks

ISBN 978 1800463 301

British Library Cataloguing in Publication Data.
A catalogue record for this book is available from the British Library.

Printed and bound in the UK by TJ Books Ltd, Padstow, Cornwall
Typeset in 11pt Bembo by Troubador Publishing Ltd, Leicester, UK

Matador is an imprint of Troubador Publishing Ltd

To Michael Ashfield MBE
For his continued interest and support

Chapter 1

I had been waiting for Lena all afternoon. Now it was well into the evening and already dark. I was mystified by her late appearance, and my telephone calls to check on her arrival had not met with success. The telephone had rung, but nobody had answered.

Now worried and concerned, I was contemplating what my next action should be, when the doorbell did at last sound with its distinctive 'ding dong'. I hurried to the door, full of excitement and expectation, my concern already starting to recede.

It was not Lena who stood on the doorstep. Instead a middle-aged man addressed me. 'Taxi, guv. Ten pounds to pay.'

I glanced in the direction of his nod and gesture. In the light of a nearby street lamp I could see a taxi standing on the road outside. I could just make out in the darkness somebody I assumed to be Lena looking out of the window in our direction.

I uttered a quick 'Just a minute', and hurried to my den to collect some money, puzzled why Lena remained sitting in the taxi. I returned with the correct cash and then, remembering that taxi drivers normally require a tip for their services, I fumbled in my pockets for some loose change, at the same time exclaiming, 'Oh – just a second.'

The taxi driver, clearly seeing what my intentions were, reacted immediately. 'That's all right, guv.'

As he swung round to return to his taxi he grinned and remarked, 'Buy the lady a pair of shoes.' With that he departed

1

down the garden path, leaving me to follow him, puzzled by his last comment...

It had all started several weeks before. I had been in London visiting my agent for one of our periodic meetings. I was heading for home, deep in thought, walking through Soho, when I heard a voice.

'Tim Mallon!'

There was no mistaking who was being addressed. The street was almost deserted, except for a few people well out of earshot. The man who had called out was sitting outside a pub on the opposite side of the street, a half-consumed glass of beer on the table in front of him. I recognised him immediately: an old face from the past and from my student days. Boris Smirnov. I guessed I had not seen him for close on three years. He was beckoning me over.

I crossed the street towards him. As I drew close he indicated the seat opposite him. 'Sit down, old boy. Have a drink.'

I hesitated. I did not really want a drink so early in the day. It was not yet midday, but politeness made me accept. 'OK,' I responded, 'but can we sit inside?' Though occasionally a weak sun was shining, the March morning was cool, and sitting outside in the chill air did not appeal to me.

'Of course. Why not?' Boris grabbed his glass and jumped up at once.

I followed him into the pub. It was dark inside and few people occupied the seating. Some sort of uninspiring music was playing quietly in the background.

Boris turned to me. 'Let me buy you a drink. What'll it be?'

'Oh. Just a half of lager,' I replied.

'Have a pint.'

I shook my head. 'Just a half,' I insisted.

Boris departed for the bar. I sought out a table in a corner, remote and quiet, from where I could study him. I hardly listed

2

him as a friend. We had been at university at the same time, but our interests had been very different and we had never had regular contact, though some of Boris's exploits occasionally put him in the spotlight. I knew he had Russian parents and spoke fluent Russian. Since leaving university we had barely seen each other. I remembered he worked in London at one of the government departments – MI5 or something like that, where, I suppose, in the cold war era we were in, his language skills were an asset.

Boris returned carrying my drink and another full pint for himself. I recalled that he had always had the ability to consume generous quantities of alcohol, very often without any apparent effect. He placed the glasses on the table and slumped into a chair opposite me. He immediately took a swig of his beer and addressed me again. 'So, what brings you to London?' He scrutinised me as I sought an answer.

'Oh, I come up from time to time to see my agent,' I replied casually, not wishing to go into details.

'Still scribing, then?' It was only half a question.

I nodded. 'It pays some of the bills.'

'You must be a millionaire by now.'

I shook my head and smiled. 'Not really. I have to do some other things as well to make a decent living.'

'I thought all authors made a lot of money.'

I shook my head again. 'It doesn't always work out like that,' I replied. For good measure I added, 'That's the opinion of the general public.' I smiled again. 'Some do and some don't. It's much the same as in any profession. It's like actors – some make it big and become household names, others just remain as supporting actors or actresses, just about earning a living.'

There was a few seconds' silence between us. Boris was clearly absorbing what I had just said, while I waited for some sort of response. He changed the subject. 'How's your wife? I've forgotten her name… Jean, is it?'

His question brought back a little bit of sadness, but I had not seen him since my divorce over two years previously. 'It didn't actually work out. Jean and I got divorced. I think she's remarried again now.'

'Sorry to hear that, old boy.'

I nodded in acknowledgement. I decided to move the conversation in another direction, not wishing to divulge the finer points of my life. I wanted to find out a bit more about Boris. 'What are you doing now?' I asked.

Boris seemed surprised by my question. 'Oh… Still working here in London. Cloak-and-dagger stuff. You know the sort of thing. Been at it for a few years now. Had a promotion last year.'

I sensed that it was a bit of a hurried reply and that Boris did not want to talk about his work life. Given what he was involved in, it was understandable. However, he volunteered another bit of information. 'My work takes me to Berlin from time to time. My German and the old family language come in handy.' He changed the subject. 'Where are you living now?'

'Ruislip,' I replied. 'I moved there after the divorce.'

A beam spread over Boris's face. 'That's not far from us. We're in Ealing.'

The 'us' bit of his comment made me curious. Ever since I had known him, Boris had never been one of those people who went overboard on permanent relationships with the opposite sex, and certainly not marriage. If his past showing was any indication, it appeared to be quite the opposite.

'Who's "us"?' I asked.

'The current girlfriend. Only been with her a short time. You'd like her. She's your type.'

'How do you mean?'

'You know. Quiet. Docile.'

I was puzzled how Boris appeared to know so much and be able to state my preference with respect to women. I opened my mouth to reply, but he butted in quickly.

'Why don't you give me your address?'

Somewhat reluctantly, I rummaged in my pocket for one of my cards. I handed it to him.

He glanced at it briefly and stuck it in the top pocket of his jacket. 'I'll give you a ring sometime,' he remarked, almost casually.

Out of courtesy I was about to ask him for his card or contact details, but he interrupted with a quick glance at his watch and, 'Sorry, old boy. I've got to go. Work calls. I only nipped out for a haircut and then fancied a drink.'

I took the hint and immediately got up from my seat, at the same time picking up and drinking the last of my lager. Boris had already consumed his pint.

I followed him outside. The sun had now come out again and was brightening things up.

Boris turned to me, grabbed my hand and shook it firmly. 'Nice seeing you again. I'll be in touch.'

'Of course,' I replied, wondering what he meant by the remark. We had never been this familiar in the past. My immediate thought was that it would most likely be another couple of years before we bumped into each other again.

Boris gave me another of his grins, uttered a brisk 'Bye', and turned on his heel to leave.

'Goodbye. Thanks for the drink,' I called after him.

He acknowledged my words with a brief wave of his hand, but did not turn round.

I started to walk. My route lay in the opposite direction.

It was well into the afternoon when I returned home. During our marriage, Jean had been earning a great deal more money than I, and we could afford a much bigger house. When we split up, the house we lived in had to be sold and the proceeds shared, and we each went our own way. I had been forced to find alternative accommodation and had purchased my present house quickly and on the spur of the moment. It was a rather dismal semi-detached property in a road of similar houses. It had been in a rather poor state when I purchased it and I had had to spend a bit of time and money making it comfortable to live in. The central heating boiler had had to be replaced and the kitchen modernised.

One bonus of this particular property was that it was within five minutes' walk of the railway station. This had proved to be so useful that in the end I had disposed of my ancient car and resorted to hiring a car when I wanted to go somewhere further afield. The decision also solved another daily irritation. The house had no garage, and parking on the road outside had become a problem. More than once I had ventured out and on my return had had to park some distance away because a lot of people left their cars in the street during the day while commuting to London by train.

As I crunched my way up the gravel path to the front door, I observed that the tiny bit of lawn that took up most of the garden needed its first cut of the year. As the day was sunny and dry, I toyed with the idea of doing the job later in the afternoon.

I let myself into the house and picked up the mail from the floor. Closing the door, I went through the usual routine of kicking off my shoes. At the same time I noticed a note left by my cleaner, Mrs Batty, advising me that I needed to buy a new toothbrush and that she would be slightly late on her next visit. I smiled to myself. My arrangement with Mrs Batty had started life as her just doing some cleaning for me. That had developed into a routine whereby she regularly worked more hours than I paid her for. On top of that she took quite an interest in my domestic equipment, regularly advising me when things needed replacing.

Still holding the mail, I wandered into the kitchen. I did not have a great deal of inclination to start work on anything. Remembering that I had not had any lunch, I made myself a cheese sandwich and mug of tea. With the mail under my arm and my hands full, I made my way into the front room. It was a room I did not use very often and as a result my choice of furniture was decidedly meagre. A second-hand three-piece suite took up much of the space, while a sideboard, also second-hand, provided a useful resting place for my hi-fi unit. Several bookshelves completed the furnishing to date.

I settled into one of the armchairs and recalled the events of the day. The meeting with my agent had gone well. He was still eager to do business when I next produced anything, which was always satisfying. Then my thoughts turned to Boris Smirnov. I had felt a certain intrigue. At Oxford our relationship had never been close, and our contact since graduating had consisted of bumping into each other at odd times. Boris was quite a unique character. While at university he had quickly adopted the public school image, which was reflected in his constantly addressing male contacts as 'old boy', which sometimes sounded odd. I pondered the fact that we had never previously exchanged addresses. It seemed strange that on this occasion Boris had almost insisted on obtaining mine, but I closed my observations with the thought once again that no doubt it would be another two years or so before we ran into each other again.

However, as events would prove, I was wrong.

Chapter 2

Two weeks had passed since my encounter with Boris Smirnov. I had been pretty busy during that time and had almost forgotten the incident.

It was on a Thursday, when I was looking forward to the weekend, that things changed. I had been planning to visit my parents in Bristol, but the weather forecast predicted strong winds and rain for that part of the country, so this created a state of uncertainty in my decision-making, as I hated driving a long distance in the rain.

I had just finished my evening meal when the telephone rang. I picked it up.

'Is that my old friend Tim Mallon? Boris Smirnov here.'

'Yes. That's me,' I confirmed, wondering what Boris had up his sleeve.

'Look here. What are you doing this weekend? Why don't you pop over and see us? You can meet Lena.'

I think it was the last sentence that perhaps persuaded me to accept the offer. I was interested to discover what kind of girl Boris had teamed up with. However, I still hesitated slightly. 'Well, I'm not sure what I'm doing this weekend. I—'

'Oh, come on, old boy. We'd love to see you.'

I conceded. 'OK. Which day and what time?'

'How about Sunday? Say, about three-ish.'

'That's fine. But I need your address.'

'Great. I'll give it to you. Got a pen?'

I grabbed the notepad and pen that I kept by the telephone. 'OK. Fire away.'

I carefully wrote down the address Boris gave me, together with a couple of tips on how to find it. 'That's fine. Got it,' I confirmed.

Boris was clearly pleased that I had accepted his invitation. 'Good. We'll look forward to that.'

'Look forward to seeing you,' I agreed, somewhat cautiously.

'Until Sunday, then,' Boris replied enthusiastically.

After putting the telephone down, I wandered into the kitchen with the washing-up in mind. The telephone call and invitation from Boris puzzled me a little. In all the years since we had left university, he had never made any contact with me. On top of that, his repeated reference to a partner appeared almost out of character. He had never come over as a person who would settle down into domestic bliss. Clearly he had changed quite a lot. The situation intrigued me.

On the Sunday, it was coming up to the agreed hour when I turned into the road where Boris and his partner lived. It was a road similar to the one I lived on, fairly quiet with a row of semi-detached houses on each side. A few parked cars on the road completed the scene. It appeared that the road did not have the same parking problem as the one I lived in, though perhaps the fact that it was a Sunday had something to do with the lack of cars. Even where I lived, parking was easier at the weekend, when the commuters did not go to work.

I quickly found the house and made my way to the front door, at the same time noticing the rather unkempt tiny front garden. I pressed the doorbell button and was aware of a bell ringing in the distance.

I waited a few minutes before the door was flung open wide and Boris stood there. He was dressed in a grubby pair of jeans and a rather crumpled shirt. 'Come in, come in!' he exclaimed, his face beaming. He stepped back to let me pass.

I entered the rather cramped hallway, which was little more than a corridor.

'Just throw your coat there,' Boris instructed, indicating a convenient chair.

I complied and followed him into the adjoining lounge. The room was reminiscent of my own, furnished quickly and with whatever could be obtained at a reasonable price to fill the emptiness. Two sofas well past their prime were centre stage, and several other chairs, the inevitable hi-fi unit and a well-worn carpet completed the furnishings.

Boris selected one of the sofas to sit on and I sat facing him on the second sofa.

'So, how was the journey?' he enquired.

'Quite good, really. It didn't take too long,' I replied.

'No car?'

I shook my head. 'There's not really any point in having one for it not to be used most of the time. I live quite near to the shops and public transport,' I explained, adding, 'Parking was always a bit of a problem.'

Boris nodded in agreement. 'Same here. OK at the weekend, pretty bad during the week,' he replied. He grinned at me. 'I suppose the answer is to buy a house with a garage.' He changed the subject. 'Tell me. You and Jean parted. What happened?'

It was something I did not really want to talk about with Boris, knowing his attitude to women. Jean and I had known each other at university. After that there had been a gap as we each pursued a career. Some time later we had met again in London and got together again. After a while we had decided to get married and set up home in Pinner. It had come as a bit of a blow when Jean came home one evening and announced that she wanted a divorce. Talking did not change her mind, and we separated by mutual consent. I moved to Ruislip and Jean eventually set up home in London with someone I had never met. Boris's question had caught me a bit off guard. My reply was brief. 'Jean met somebody else.'

'Sorry about that, old boy.'

I nodded in reply, but I now wanted to ask Boris a question and satisfy my curiosity, one of the reasons I had accepted his invitation. 'What about you?' I asked. 'From your remark when we met a few weeks ago it sounds as if you have entered the field of domestic bliss.'

The response from Boris was almost what I expected. 'What? No way! I'm not going to be tied down by some whining, whingeing female.'

I was about to reply, but he suddenly stood up and looked at me. 'Want a coffee?' he enquired.

'That would be great,' I answered.

Boris immediately went over to the door and opened it halfway before bellowing, 'Lena... LENA!'

There was a distant reply from another room.

Boris returned to his seat. 'She won't be a minute,' he declared.

Almost immediately the door was pushed open and a slim, fair-haired young woman entered. She looked enquiringly at Boris, clearly expecting some instructions.

'Get us some coffee,' Boris ordered – rather harshly, I felt. Almost as an afterthought, he added, addressing me, 'This is Lena.' He then spoke again to Lena. 'This is Tim, an old friend of mine.'

For almost the first time, Lena looked at me and gave a tiny smile. She took the few steps towards me and held out her hand. Her greeting as she took my outstretched hand was again accompanied by that smile.

'Hello, Lena,' I said cheerily.

'Coffee with sugar and milk?' she asked. Her voice had a slight accent, the origin of which was difficult to ascertain.

'Black, please, with no sugar,' I replied.

She nodded and turned to leave the room.

11

I watched her go. The clothes she was wearing puzzled me. She was dressed in some sort of kaftan, which completely enveloped her. On her feet she had a pair of tatty plimsolls without any laces. It seemed such an odd way for a clearly attractive girl to dress.

As she closed the door, Boris turned to me. 'She's Polish. She can't speak much English.'

'How long has she been with you?' I asked.

'Oh, only a couple of months,' he replied, casually. He looked at me with a grin. 'You know me. Never keep my wenches long.' He nodded in the direction of the door. 'I'm due for a change.'

His final remark horrified me a bit. I had always known about his attitude to women, but this seemed so cold and calculating. I wondered how the two of them had got together in the first place.

'Where did you meet her?' I asked.

Boris looked at me almost as if he expected the question. 'Berlin,' he replied quickly.

I had a feeling that he did not want to pursue this topic. I decided to change the direction of our exchange. 'How long have you been living here?'

He thought for a second. 'A year and a… No, almost two years. It's not in very good repair. Needs a lot of work and money spent on it. Last winter the roof leaked.'

'How are your parents?' I asked, keeping the conversation going.

'Oh they're OK. Still living in the East End. Dad's getting a bit frail now, but Mum's full of beans. I saw them a week or so ago.'

I was about to reply, but Boris beat me to it. 'What about yours?' he asked.

'They're both fine,' I replied. I felt I had to embellish my reply. 'I was going to go and see them this weekend, but the weather down there is pretty awful at the moment.'

'Where is "down there"?'

'They moved to Bristol several years ago. They are both from there originally,' I explained.

Our almost formal chatting was interrupted by the return of Lena, who was carrying two mugs of coffee on a tray. She handed me mine with again that pleasant smile. I noticed her delicate hands as she passed me the mug. She immediately left the room again. I watched her walk away, closing the door behind her. It seemed odd that she did not join us.

Boris took a sip of his coffee and the next instant gave a sigh of exasperation. 'This damn coffee is cold!' he exclaimed. He looked at me enquiringly. 'What's yours like?'

I tasted my coffee. 'Mine's fine,' I said.

Boris muttered something under his breath and the next instant bellowed out again, 'LENA!' Lena reappeared almost immediately, as if she had been waiting for the summons. 'This coffee's cold,' Boris growled, holding the mug out in her direction.

Lena flushed visibly. 'Oh, I am so sorry. I will make you another one.' She took the mug from him and hurried from the room.

I was surprised and quite shocked by Boris's reaction and his treatment of Lena over such a trivial matter. I felt I had to express my feelings. 'You were a bit hard on her,' I remarked.

Boris shook his head. 'The only treatment some women understand,' he retorted.

I did not answer and it did not take long for Lena to reappear with the replacement mug of coffee. She handed it to Boris and waited anxiously. He tested the coffee and just gave out one word: 'OK.' Lena immediately turned on her heel and left the room again without saying a word.

As a way of changing the subject, I turned my attention to a painting that hung on the wall opposite me. It was a watercolour of an English country scene, light and airy, in contrast to the two other pictures in the room, which were Russian scenes painted in oils.

'I like the painting,' I remarked, nodding in the direction of my interest.

'I detest it,' Boris snorted.

I continued to direct my gaze at the painting. I became taken up with the scene it depicted. It needed a different frame, I concluded. The horrid silver one did nothing to enhance it.

I was surprised by Boris's next remark. 'Do you want it?' he asked enthusiastically.

It did not take me long to answer. 'I do like it,' I replied, still looking at it.

'Take it with you,' he offered. 'It'll cost you a bottle of wine,' he added with a grin.

'Done. That would be fine with me. Thank you very much.' My acceptance was firm and positive.

'Take it today,' Boris urged.

I shook my head. 'Not in this. I don't want to risk getting it damaged.' I nodded towards the window, where the rain had started once again, beating on the windowpane.

'Come again next week and pick it up, then.'

'Yes, I could do that,' I replied.

Our conversation turned to our university days. My own experience had been very different from that of Boris, who had indulged in the high life. It was strange how he had found time to do any studying.

We chatted for the best part of an hour, and then I made an excuse to take my leave, explaining that I had something else to attend to. Boris did not try to persuade me to stay longer, and I was glad of that.

As we went into the hall again, after picking up my coat I glanced towards what I supposed was the kitchen door and where I guessed Lena was.

'Goodbye, Lena,' I called out.

The kitchen door opened and Lena peeped out. She smiled at me and almost whispered, 'Goodbye.'

Boris, meanwhile, had opened the front door. I turned to leave.

He grinned at me. 'Cheerio. Nice seeing you, old boy.'

'Thank you for the coffee,' I replied. 'See you next week.'

With that, I departed, and Boris closed the door behind me.

As I walked away, I turned and looked back at the house. Boris had been correct in his description. Compared to its neighbours, it certainly looked tatty and in need of some care – first and foremost a good coat of paint.

I made my way home, reflecting on the experience. For some reason my thoughts returned again and again to Lena. Boris's attitude towards her had been diabolical. I knew from my university days that his regard for women was not very high, but in the case of Lena the situation puzzled me. It seemed odd that such an attractive girl should allow herself to be subjected to the kind of treatment I had witnessed during my visit. I wondered why she did not leave him. There were many questions attached to their relationship, but few answers. Perhaps more information would be gleaned when I returned to collect the painting. In a way, I was glad I had an excuse to pay Boris and Lena another visit.

Chapter 3

On the Wednesday following my visit to Boris, just as I was settling down for the evening, I received another telephone call from him.

He did not waste time on formalities, but came straight to the point. 'Look here, old boy, are you coming over this weekend?'

'Well, we talked about it,' I replied.

'You must come. I want to talk to you.'

'What about?'

'I'll tell you when I see you.'

'Why the secrecy?'

'I'll explain all when I see you.'

It was clear that I was not going to get any more out of Boris at this stage. I decided to make the call short. 'OK. I can come over on Sunday afternoon.'

'Fine. Make it three o'clock. Don't be late.'

'I'll try not to be. Bye for now.'

'See you then.'

With that he was gone. I put the phone down. The call puzzled me. What was Boris up to that necessitated a special call with such a mystery attached to it? The more I thought about it, the more intrigued I became.

On the Sunday the weather was fine and sunny. It was a situation that pleased me greatly, as I knew that transporting the picture in inclement weather conditions would present problems. Just in case, I took with me a waterproof sheet. It nestled in my rucksack with the two bottles of wine needed to complete the deal.

On this particular trip, the public transport was better than I had anticipated and I ended up arriving much earlier than Boris and I had agreed. I wondered if I should try to kill time somewhere and then decided that I knew him well enough not to wait. I also knew from my previous visit that no special arrangements would be made for me.

I walked as slowly as possible, but even so I arrived on the doorstep almost twenty-five minutes early. I rang the bell and waited, expecting Boris to open the door. It seemed a long time before it opened. It was not Boris who stood there. It was Lena.

She looked at me for a second or two, and then recognition dawned. She swung the door wide open and stood aside for me to enter.

'Please come in,' she said.

'I'm a bit early,' I explained apologetically.

'It doesn't matter. Please come in.' The request was accompanied with a nice smile.

Lena closed the door. I spied a coat rack tucked into a corner and hung my raincoat on it, and then I followed her into the lounge. She was still dressed in the kaftan, but this time she was barefoot. Her small white feet were a sharp contrast to the drab garment. Her hair, which looked as if it had just been brushed, now fell around her shoulders. I thought she looked very attractive.

I followed her indication and sat down on one of the settees. I expected her to immediately leave the room as on the previous occasion, but this time she perched on the edge of the settee opposite me, her feet close together and her hands on her lap.

There was a brief silence between us. I was wondering how we would conduct a conversation, since Boris had told me that her English was very limited. I knew she had lived in Berlin, so I assumed she spoke German. It was a language I had picked up during a brief period working in Germany, but I had not used it for some time and I was now unsure if I could hold a detailed conversation in it.

I need not have worried. It was Lena who spoke first – in fluent English. 'Boris won't be very long. He had to go out for something.'

I was puzzled. 'But your English is excellent. Boris told me you didn't speak it very well.'

Lena gave a little smile. 'He tells everybody that.'

I was even more puzzled. I was determined to find out as much as I could about her before Boris returned. 'Boris also told me that you were Polish,' I said.

Lena replied immediately. 'My mother was Polish and I was born in Poland, but now I live in Germany and I am a German citizen.' She added quickly, 'I left Poland when I was quite small.'

'I see. Well, that explains everything,' I replied.

It was Lena who asked the next question. 'Have you known Boris a long time?'

'We were at the same university at the same time.' I explained. I felt I needed to add, 'I don't know him very well. Since our university days, we just bump into each other occasionally.'

'Boris talks a lot about you. He tells me lots of nice things about you.'

I gave a smile. 'That's good to hear,' I replied.

Never having been close to Boris, I did wonder where he got his information from to relay to Lena.

I wanted to learn more about her. 'How did you come to be in England with Boris?' I asked.

Lena hesitated, and then spoke quietly. 'I was living in Berlin. Boris met me and asked me to come here with him. Now I wish I hadn't.'

'Why?' I responded quickly, eager to know the reason.

Lena was silent for a few seconds, as if she was figuring out a suitable reply. When she did speak it was in a very low voice. 'Sometimes he is not very nice to me.'

'In what way?' I asked, determined to find out more about their relationship.

'He gets angry with me.' She hesitated again. 'Sometimes he beats me. I have marks.' She touched her back as if to draw attention to that area.

'You mean bruises?' I exclaimed.

Lena nodded. 'Yes.'

'If things are so bad, why don't you leave him?'

Lena looked at me. She seemed to be close to tears. 'I cannot. I have no papers. If the police find me, they will arrest me and put me in prison.'

'You mean you're here illegally?'

Lena nodded.

I wondered how Boris had got her into the country without documents, but that was a question for later. In the meantime I responded to her last revelation. 'I'm sure it's a problem that can be overcome,' I replied.

Lena was still almost in tears as she spoke again. She was nervously playing with a handkerchief in her lap. 'I cannot leave. He took all my money and…' She hesitated. 'And all my clothes, everything.'

That explained why she wore the same plain garment, but the disclosure shocked me. My opinion of Boris had now sunk even lower.

I was about to reply, but at that instant there was the sound of the front door opening and then being slammed shut. A few seconds later Boris entered the room. His eyes fixed on me, and then on Lena. 'Oh! You're here,' he remarked.

'Sorry. I was a bit early,' I replied, feeling that an explanation was required.

Lena had jumped up on Boris's sudden entrance. Boris gave her a quick glance. 'Get us some coffee.' She left the room without a word.

Boris sat down opposite me.

To kick off the conversation, I opened up my rucksack and removed the two bottles of wine I had brought. I placed them on a nearby table. 'Payment as agreed.'

Boris was surprised. 'Two bottles! Thank you. I'll enjoy those.' He suddenly jumped up, marched over to the painting, which was still hanging on the wall, and carefully removed it. He carried it over to me and propped it up against the settee. 'Bit dusty,' he remarked with a grin, as he brushed his hands and sat down again. I noticed that there was a definite mark on the wall where the picture had hung. I wondered vaguely if the painting had been there before Boris bought the house. Perhaps that was why he didn't like it.

'I'll sort it out,' I replied.

'I'm just glad to see the back of it,' Boris chuckled, suddenly answering my private thought. 'It was on the wall when I bought this place. I bought some things from the previous owner and he threw some things in, including that.' He nodded in the direction of the painting.

At that instant Lena reappeared with two mugs of coffee. Once again she disappeared as quickly as she had arrived, without speaking. I noticed that this time she was wearing the ghastly shoes without laces.

I sipped my coffee. 'Why doesn't Lena sit with us?' I asked.

Boris gave me one of his grins. 'She's well trained,' he replied.

It appeared to me to be an odd arrangement, and my conversation with Lena earlier was very much uppermost in my mind. It appeared as if Boris had some sort of hold over her that she was unable to do anything about. I was also curious to know why Boris wanted to see me. It looked as if I was going to have to bring up the subject. 'What did you want to talk to me about?' I asked.

Boris looked at me for a couple of seconds without speaking. He took a gulp of coffee and continued to look at me intently before making a reply. 'You're attracted to Lena.'

I wasn't sure if the remark was a question or a statement. Either way it came as a bit of a shock. 'What makes you say that?' I replied, forcing myself to adopt a casual approach.

'Don't deny it. You can't keep your eyes off her.'

I bristled at the statement. Even if it was true, I did not like to be confronted in such a manner. 'You sound very sure of yourself. I don't know how you came to that conclusion.'

Boris gave me another of his grins. 'Look, old boy. Don't let's fall out over my observation. Let's talk about it man to man. You fancy Lena and I want to get rid of her. How about you taking up with her?'

The suggestion came as a bolt from the blue. Boris had clearly planned everything in detail. I felt I had to play things casually.

I gave a bit of a grin. 'You're missing one vital point,' I remarked.

'What's that?'

'You assuming Lena would want to be part of such an arrangement.'

'She is willing, and I have little doubt that earlier she told you about all her woes.'

I decided to try another tactic. 'Anyway, aren't you forgetting something?' I asked. I paused, to ensure I had Boris's full attention before continuing. 'She's here in this country illegally. She has no papers.'

I could see that my comment irritated him. His reply was quick. 'How do you know that? Oh, I suppose she told you.' He was silent for a second or two. 'Anyway, that's not a major problem. It can be got over quite easily. You can sort it out.'

'You sound very sure. Lena and I might both get arrested,' I pointed out. 'And I wouldn't know how to begin to get papers for her.'

Boris shook his head. 'I doubt if you'd be arrested for that. Anyway, I might be able to help you with getting her here legally – you know, pull a few strings…'

He appeared to have covered every obstacle in his plan. There was silence between us for a few seconds.

The slightly uncomfortable atmosphere was broken by Boris. 'Consider my suggestion as a short-term interlude,' he proposed.

'Just like you did.' I couldn't help saying it.

Boris appeared unperturbed by my sarcastic remark. 'Of course. Why not? Anyway, she'll want to return to Germany soon enough.'

Our conversation, such as it was, was interrupted by Lena, who re-entered the room.

For once Boris was a bit more conciliatory towards her. 'Tell Tim you're agreeable to going to stay with him and warm his bed,' he said.

Lena looked at me. She was a bit flushed. 'Yes. I am willing,' she answered quietly.

'There you are.' Boris spoke more to me than to Lena.

I decided it was time to change the way things were going. Glancing down at the painting, I announced my intention. 'I must wrap this up.' I reached into my rucksack for the plastic sheet.

'I can help you,' Lena offered eagerly.

Together we carefully protected the painting, Lena kneeling on the floor. She was in fact better at the job than I was. All the time we were watched by Boris, who said nothing.

When we had finished, Lena jumped up and with a quick smile at me collected the empty coffee mugs and left the room.

'There you are,' announced Boris again as soon as she was gone.

I was not sure what his words were supposed to mean, and I made no reply.

'So, what about it?' Boris was clearly not going to give up.

'I'll think about it.' I was not going to make a hasty decision.

'Don't leave it too long.'

I nodded but made no reply.

'I'll give you a call in a few days.'

'Yes. Give me few days. I have to make some arrangements,' I replied, thinking about the spare bedroom, which I would have to clear of junk if my answer was to be in the affirmative.

Boris seemed to accept my decision, and for the rest of my short stay we talked about other things, mostly our university days and the other students we had shared life with there.

When I felt it was time to go, I made a move to leave, picking up the carefully packaged painting. I could just about carry it under my arm. Boris took my hint and led me into the hall, making his way to the front door and opening it wide. It was at this point that Lena appeared from the kitchen. She was full of smiles and to my surprise she came straight up to me, grabbed my hand and planted a kiss on my cheek. 'Goodbye – and thank you,' she said.

I left the house quickly. The weather had turned much warmer and I was well on my way home before I realised that I had left my raincoat in Boris's house. At that point, I was unaware how and when I would next see it. I would find out in a rather unexpected way.

Chapter 4

Several days after my visit to Boris, I was still undecided about Lena. I think the reason for this was that I objected to being manipulated by Boris. On the other hand, I felt sorry for Lena. It seemed strange that a mature young woman, who she clearly was, could have allowed herself to be completely controlled by Boris. There seemed to be a mystery attached to the situation. It intrigued me. On top of that, I had to admit that I was attracted to Lena.

It seemed a strange predicament to be in. Even if I submitted to Boris's persuasion, I did not know if I was acquiring a new girlfriend and bedfellow, or a lodger for a few days or weeks until Lena decided to return home to Germany. It was an odd position to be in and not one I particularly liked. In a way it was completely out of character for me, yet at the same time I felt that I could not push things away. I played for time by waiting for Boris to contact me rather than making a move myself. I was confident that he would get in touch sooner rather than later.

Somehow I summoned up the enthusiasm to clear out the clutter in my spare bedroom and make it a bit more welcoming. It was a kind of 'just in case' action. Though my house had three bedrooms, the second-largest had never been furnished. If required, I could always use the smallest, as it contained a single bed, in use infrequently when somebody wanted to stay for the night. As a result, I had acquired the habit of dumping items in there out of sight. Most of the time, the bedding remained unused in my airing cupboard, carefully laundered and placed there by Mrs Batty, who readily made up the bed for me when I mentioned that I might be having an overnight guest. I even found a pair of pyjamas a female guest had left behind and never collected, washed and neatly ironed by Mrs Batty. I recalled that the guest had been about the same size as Lena.

On the Wednesday evening the telephone rang. Somehow I had the feeling it would be Boris. However, I was not quite correct. It was a woman's voice at the other end of the line.

'This is Lena.'

'Lena!' My voice registered surprised and pleasure.

She spoke again. 'Please can I come and stay with you? PLEASE.' I detected anxiety and urgency in her voice.

The next instant I heard Boris. 'You heard the lady. Is it a yes?'

I had never had to make a decision so fast. Somehow, the tone of Lena's voice had made it for me. I just uttered one word: 'OK.'

'Splendid. I'll send her over tomorrow.'

'Not tomorrow.' I suddenly remembered that I had an appointment.

'Friday, then. I'll make the arrangements.'

'I'll come and fetch her,' I replied quickly.

'Don't worry. I'll send her over in a taxi in the afternoon.'

I made no reply to the suggestion. In a way it suited me, as I could now spend a little more time getting ready for my new guest.

Suddenly I thought of something. 'My raincoat. I left it on your coat rack. Can you ask Lena to bring it with her when she comes?'

'Will do, old boy. Must go now.'

With that, the telephone went dead.

So the die was cast. Lena was coming to stay with me. Now that a decision had been made, I was quite looking forward to having her in my home, whether as a lodger or as a bed companion. Since my divorce, female company had been sadly lacking in my life.

I awoke early on the Friday. The weather had a rather dark and gloomy look about it, and there was a hint of rain in the air. After a quick breakfast, I decided to make a visit to the supermarket and top up on some basic items like tea, coffee and milk, plus some extra food. I did not want to run out of anything while I had a guest to entertain.

I was quite excited and at the same time intrigued about having Lena to stay. There were a lot of questions I wanted to ask her so that I could perhaps find out more about her strange relationship with Boris.

As soon as I returned from my shopping outing, I spent a little time just doing a few odd jobs around the house, making it more attractive for a female guest. While I was out I had even bought some flowers and these now occupied a central position in my lounge. By lunchtime I was quite satisfied with all my efforts.

During the afternoon, while waiting for Lena's arrival, I busied myself doing some work in my den. I felt I needed to keep the next day or so free, so that I could spend some time with my new companion.

Mid afternoon came and went, the day headed towards evening, and still there was no sign of Lena. Unsure what to do, all I could do was wait.

I felt greatly relieved when the taxi driver eventually called at the house to announce her arrival. Still puzzled by his remark about buying her a pair of shoes, I quickly followed him to the taxi.

When he opened the door I could see Lena sitting on the back seat looking nervous. I smiled at her reassuringly. 'Hello, Lena. It's nice to see you. Come on into the house.'

As she moved to climb out of the taxi, I received a bit of a shock. She was wearing my raincoat. And the taxi driver had been right. She had nothing on her feet.

The day had been cool for the end of March. Now the evening was damp and inclement. I had come out in haste without putting on a coat and now felt the chill in the air. 'Quick, let's get you into the warm,' I urged.

With a nod and a brief thank you to the taxi driver, I led the way to the house. I was surprised that Lena did not appear to have any luggage, although she was clutching a rather tatty plastic supermarket bag. As we walked slowly the dozen or so yards to the front door, I noticed her wince several times as her bare feet encountered the sharp gravel on the path. I wondered why she was not wearing the horrible plimsolls I had seen on her feet on my visits to Boris's house.

We entered the hall, with its welcoming bright light. I closed the front door and turned to Lena, who stood there looking quite miserable. 'Let me take the coat,' I offered, making a move to help her off with it.

Her reaction was swift, and automatic. She immediately clutched the coat close to her. She uttered a hoarse 'No' and looked at me in alarm.

I stopped dead, startled at how she had reacted to my offer of help. There were tears in her eyes as she looked at me.

She spoke in almost a whisper. 'I have no clothes.'

For a second I could not summon up any response. I did not immediately grasp what she was conveying.

She spoke again in a subdued voice. 'He made me do it.'

I still struggled to comprehend what was happening. It was obvious that Lena was referring to Boris, but I had to have clarification of what he had done. 'You mean Boris made you come here naked with only my coat to wear?'

Lena nodded but said nothing. Anger welled up inside me. How could Boris carry out such a despicable act?

Lena still stood looking dejected. She interrupted my thoughts about Boris. Still clutching the coat about her, she whispered, 'I am so cold.'

I reacted immediately. 'Of course. You must be freezing. Come on. It's warmer in here.'

I made a move towards the kitchen, where the boiler was burning. Lena followed me, still looking lost and almost bewildered.

'Would you like some soup?' I asked. I had not eaten since midday and I suddenly remembered the soup Mrs Batty had made for me and left in the fridge. It was just one of the little odd jobs she did for me.

Lena nodded and replied softly, 'Yes, please.'

'Please sit down,' I urged. 'I'll just warm it up.'

Lena sat down at the table. She looked miserable. I felt I had to make an attempt to get her talking while I prepared the soup.

'I thought you might come over earlier in the day,' I enquired.

Lena shook her head. 'I wanted to come sooner, but Boris made me do things for him.'

'Why did he make you come without any clothes?'

Lena looked up at me. She was almost in tears again. 'He said you would enjoy it. He laughed about it. When I refused he beat me.'

Again the anger welled up inside me. I had to make my feelings known to Lena. 'Well, I did not appreciate it and I am angry with Boris for making you do it,' I responded.

Lena did not reply. She looked at me as if trying to establish whether I meant what I said.

I suddenly thought of something else. 'We need to get your clothes. I'll phone Boris after we've eaten.'

Lena shook her head. 'I don't know what he did with them. He took everything, even my shoes, so that I couldn't go out of the house.'

'You mean you were a prisoner?' I asked, shocked by the disclosure.

She nodded. 'Yes.'

Lena's revelation not only shocked me, but also confirmed my opinion of Boris. Since I had known him, he had always had an odd way of treating the women in his life. Something that had taken place during our university days had been an early indication of this. Following one of Boris's all-night parties, a female student had been found in the early morning tied to a lamp post close to the university. She had been in a maximum state of undress. Evidence had led to Boris being the instigator. It looked as if he would be sent down. Luckily for him, the girl involved refused to openly accuse him, with the result that he survived with a severe reprimand.

This incident came back to me as I pondered Boris's current conduct. At the same time there still seemed to be unanswered questions about Lena's relationship with him. Why had she allowed all those things to happen and accepted his extreme treatment of her? I was determined to get the answers in due course. In the meantime there were other things to attend to.

I finished heating the soup and divided it into two bowls. I remembered the rolls I had purchased that morning and placed them on the kitchen table, together with the butter and some cheese.

I sat down opposite Lena. For the most part we ate in silence, each lost in our own thoughts.

Towards the end of the meal I tried to resume some sort of conversation. 'How long have you been with Boris?'

'Two months.' Lena did not look up from the table.

'Was he unkind to you most of the time?'

Lena nodded. 'Yes.'

Eventually we finished our simple meal. Lena was sitting huddled in my raincoat. Ever since her arrival I had been desperately thinking about what I could give her to wear. Vaguely I wondered if Mrs Batty could help. She only lived at the end of the road, and though she was much bigger than Lena she did have two daughters who might be closer to Lena's size.

Lena interrupted my thoughts. 'I am still cold. Can I have a hot bath, please?'

I jumped up immediately. 'Of course you can,' I replied, mentally kicking myself for not suggesting it earlier.

I led her upstairs. I grabbed a large fluffy bath towel from the airing cupboard and handed it to her. So far she had not spoken again, but suddenly she asked, 'Where will I sleep?'

It was something I had been considering. I still did not know whether I had a lodger or a bedfellow.

I answered carefully. 'That's where I sleep,' I replied casually, indicating my room. 'There's this room as well,' I added, pushing open the door of the spare room.

Lena did not reply. I opened the door to the bathroom and switched on the light. 'Here you are. The water should be nice and hot.'

Lena gave me a hint of a smile as she uttered a polite 'Thank you'.

'Enjoy your bath,' I said cheerily as I turned to leave her and retreat downstairs. I had a telephone call to make.

I carefully dialled Boris's number.

He answered almost immediately. 'Hello.'

'Boris, it's Tim.'

I did not waste time on fineries. I plunged straight in. 'What the blazes do you think you're about, sending Lena over practically naked? Did you want her to get pneumonia?'

'I thought you'd enjoy that.'

'Well, I didn't, and I don't think much of you for doing it.'

'Sorry about that.' There was no indication of remorse in his tone.

I realised I was not going to get anywhere further with him, in spite of my anger towards him. Besides, there were more pressing things to attend to.

'Look, she needs clothes. I'm coming over right away to pick some up.' I had already figured out that I would use a taxi to get me there and back quickly.

'Can't be done, old boy. I'm just about to go to Germany.'

30

'Can't you just wait twenty minutes, until I can get to you?'

'Sorry, I've got a plane to catch.'

'But—' I started to protest, but he cut me short.

'Got to go. My taxi's here. Talk to you later.'

The line went dead.

Feeling extremely irritated, I wandered back into the kitchen. A big problem was slowly getting larger and larger. How was I going to fix Lena up with clothing? Various ideas and options flowed through my thoughts, but each one boiled down to not being practical.

I made a pot of tea and poured myself a cup, which I drank slowly while glancing through the newspaper I had not had time to peruse during the day. I could hear Lena in the bathroom above me.

What seemed to be a long time passed before everything went quiet. I expected Lena to reappear, but when she did not I decided to investigate. I crept quietly up the stairs, careful avoiding the step that gave a loud creak. The bathroom was slightly ajar, the light switched off. The door to the spare room was open, but the bed was empty. The pair of pyjamas I had left on it for Lena to wear had disappeared. I pushed the door of my own room open. Lena was in the bed. She appeared to be asleep. So the answer to my previous question had been answered. Lena did not consider herself to be just a lodger.

I took my time in the bathroom getting ready for bed. When I eventually crept into the bedroom, Lena was still apparently sleeping. As carefully as I could, I climbed into bed. She did not stir.

I lay awake for a long time. It seemed odd to be sharing a bed again. Lena slept peacefully, though occasionally she murmured something I could not make out in her sleep. One question was now uppermost in my mind: how was I going to solve the problem of getting her some clothes? I fell asleep pondering the options open to me.

Chapter 5

It was well past my usual rising time when I at last woke up after a restless night. The space beside me was empty. Vaguely I could hear some activity in the kitchen below me. I lay there for a while.

I was about to get up when I heard footsteps coming up the stairs. Lena entered the room carrying a mug. She was wearing what I immediately observed was my white dressing gown, which usually hung unused behind the bathroom door. In a direct contrast to the previous evening, she was smiling.

'Good morning. I've brought you some tea,' she announced.

'Good morning, Lena. That's great,' I replied. It had been years since anybody had brought me tea in bed.

Lena moved to hand me the mug. 'Do you take sugar?' she asked, perhaps a little anxiously. 'If you do, I will fetch some.'

I shook my head and smiled at her. 'No, that's fine. I don't take sugar.'

Instead of leaving, she sat down on the end of the bed. She carefully and modestly arranged the dressing gown around her, her face solemn.

When she spoke, it was in a low voice. 'I am so sorry about last night.'

She looked at me rather sorrowfully, as if wanting me to understand. Before I could respond, she continued speaking. 'I was so tired. The night before, Boris kept me awake all night. He made me do things. He was not very nice to me.'

Once again, my anger against Boris raised itself. My regard for him had now sunk pretty low. I felt waves of sympathy and admiration for Lena.

She had now averted her eyes and appeared lost in her own thoughts.

'It's all right. Really, it is,' I replied. 'I understand.'

She looked at me again. She gave me a little smile and whispered softly, 'Thank you.' It was a more cheerful Lena who then asked, 'What do you have for breakfast?'

I was still sipping my tea. 'Muesli,' I replied.

'And tea?'

I nodded and grinned. 'Yes, please.'

'I am getting quite used to tea,' Lena remarked, thoughtfully. 'I will have tea as well.'

Suddenly she jumped up. 'I will get breakfast,' she announced, and with another smile and a wave of her hand she was gone.

I finished the tea, sprang out of bed and made my way to the bathroom. Taking my time, I washed and shaved, still pondering over the relationship between Lena and Boris. Clearly it appeared that she had not enjoyed her time with him, yet she had stayed and put up with all his demands and the humiliation. There still seemed to be a mystery in there somewhere. Perhaps in due course I would get the answer. In the meantime there were more pressing issues to attend to. The first was to get some clothing for Lena. I had now rejected the idea of enlisting Mrs Batty's help. Instead I would ring my old friend Pippa and get her to assist.

Twenty minutes later I made my way downstairs. As I entered the kitchen I was in for a surprise. The table had been laid and a bowl of muesli was at each end, accompanied by a mug and all the necessary cutlery. As I entered, Lena, teapot in hand, was brewing the tea.

She smiled at me again. 'Everything is ready,' she announced.

I sat down in my usual place. Lena put the pot of tea on the table. It was a departure from my usual method of making drinks: normally my tea was brewed in a mug.

Lena sat down opposite me. Suddenly she glanced down at what she was wearing, and said anxiously, 'I borrowed your dressing gown. I hope you do not mind.'

I shook my head. 'Not at all. Please help yourself. I don't wear it that often.' I brought up the problem that had been in my thoughts ever since I woke up. 'Today we need to get you fixed up with some clothes.'

'If you can lend me some money, I will go and buy some,' Lena replied. 'I will pay you back,' she added quickly.

'But you'll need something to wear to go shopping,' I pointed out.

Lena pondered my statement. It was clear that she had not thought out the details of her proposal.

I chipped in before she could reply. 'I have a friend I was at university with. She is about your size. She doesn't live too far away, so after breakfast I'll give her a call and ask her to help out.'

I could see immediately that Lena was not too keen on the idea, but it was the only solution I could think of. I just hoped that Pippa would be at home when I telephoned.

We did not refer to the subject for the rest of breakfast. Instead Lena asked me a lot of questions about my domestic arrangements, and I found it remarkable that she showed such an interest.

As soon as we had finished eating, Lena collected the dirty dishes and put them in the sink, clearly intent on doing the washing-up. I made my way to the telephone. Pippa was an artist and mainly worked at home, so there was a good chance of catching her.

I carefully dialled her number. The telephone rang for a long time. I had almost accepted the fact that she could not be at home when there was an answer.

'Yes. Hello.' It was Pippa, but her voice was muffled.

'Pippa, it's Tim – Tim Mallon.'

'What do you want at this time in the morning? I'm still in bed.' Her tone was hardly encouraging.

I suddenly remembered that Pippa was never at her best first thing in the morning. I could tell from her voice that she was still half asleep. Nevertheless, I was determined to proceed with my mission. Circumstances dictated the issue.

'Pippa,' I began, 'I'm sorry to disturb you, but I need your help.'

I heard her stifle a yawn. 'This had better be good. Waking me up in the middle of the night!'

I smiled to myself. It was already half past nine.

Before I could reply, she spoke again. 'What do you want, anyway?'

I took a deep breath. Now for it, I thought. 'I need some women's clothes.'

'WHAT?' Pippa was wide awake now.

'I'll explain everything, but I do need your help. I need a full set of women's clothing.'

'I didn't know you were into that sort of thing.' Pippa was more her normal self now.

'It's not like that. It's just that I've got a young lady here who has nothing to wear.'

'You mean she's starkers? What did you do, rip her clothes off? You should take more care!'

This was the Pippa of old talking, but I knew I still had to get round her somehow. 'Pippa, I really do need your help.'

She muttered a reply, almost to herself. 'I've got to see and hear this!'

I repeated my request. 'Pippa, help me out – please.'

Next instant there was a sort of sigh at the other end of the telephone, followed by a weary 'OK. Because it's you. But it'll cost you.'

I began to feel more cheerful. 'That's all right. Name your price.'

'Hmm… A slap-up meal somewhere?'

'Great. You're on. Can you bring the clothes over straight away?'

There was a slight hesitation at the other end.

'Please,' I urged. 'I really am stuck.'

I heard her sigh again. 'OK. I'll be over in about an hour. Put the kettle on. I'll need a coffee.' Suddenly she added, 'And this had better be a good story.'

'Fine.'

'What size is the victim, anyway?'

I thought for a second. 'She's slim, medium height. About your size.'

There was another sigh. 'OK. I'll see you shortly. Get that kettle on.' The next instant the line went dead as she put the phone down.

I replaced my handset and breathed a sigh of relief. Thanks to Pippa it looked as if the immediate problem had been solved. I knew I could depend on her. Although she often put on a rather flippant air, I knew from old that she was reliable. She had followed university with art school and now appeared to be doing quite well for herself in commercial art. In our early days we had shared a bed, but that was a long time ago and now our relationship was more like that of a brother and sister. Occasionally, when we ran across each other, I would take her out for a meal and we would exchange news of our activities. Pippa had never married, and the last time we discussed the subject it appeared that she now preferred intimate relationships with women rather than men. I had not seen her recently, so I didn't know whether that was just a passing phase or something more permanent.

As soon as I had finished talking to Pippa I went to tell Lena the news. She was not in the kitchen. I made my way upstairs and found her in the bedroom, making the bed. She looked up as I entered the room.

'Good news,' I announced. 'My friend Pippa is coming over right away with some clothes for you.'

Lena simply said, 'Thank you.' I could see that she still did not like the idea very much, but there was really no other way unless I ventured out and purchased some clothes for her.

We made bits of conversation and then I left her in the bedroom and returned downstairs. While waiting for Pippa to arrive I busied myself with several routine jobs. It was almost an hour later when I saw Pippa's sports car draw up outside. I watched her emerge and pull out a large plastic bag. The next minute she was playing a tune on the doorbell. I hurried to open the door.

'Hi,' was her cheerful greeting. She was clearly back to her old self after her earlier grumpiness at being woken up. She walked into the hall and looked around her. 'Where's the victim?' she asked.

I frowned at her. 'Don't call her that,' I replied hastily in a hushed voice, though at the same time I was grinning. I called upstairs. 'Lena, Pippa's here.'

A few seconds later Lena made her way down the stairs, looking a bit anxious.

I made brief introductions. 'Lena, this is Pippa. Pippa, meet Lena.'

Lena held out her hand with a quiet 'Hello'. Pippa gave her usual 'Hi'.

The next instant Pippa took control. Her shoes were kicked into a corner of the hall and, grabbing Lena's arm, she propelled her towards the stairs with the words 'Come with me'. And then, glancing over her shoulder, she addressed me. 'You, get the coffee going.'

I smiled to myself. That was Pippa. What you saw was what you got.

I wandered into the kitchen and put the kettle on to boil. It only seemed a few minutes before Pippa reappeared.

She sat down at the table and looked at me rather bemusedly. 'Darling, she's quite sweet. Where did you find her?'

I knew I had to confide in Pippa. I sat down at the table opposite her and started to explain. 'Do you remember Boris, who was at university at the same time as us…?'

Pippa listened intently while I went through the events of the last few days. When I had finished she took a deep breath. 'Be careful, Tim. You could get yourself into something deep.'

'I know. But at the same time I felt that I had to give Lena a roof over her head. I couldn't stand by and let Boris turn her out onto the street.'

'What about this business of her being in the country illegally?' Pippa asked, looking at me enquiringly.

I nodded. 'That's another thing. I don't know how that can be sorted out.'

Pippa was silent for a minute, thinking. Suddenly she spoke again. 'Do you remember Patrick Jenson, who was with us at university?

'Yes, I do.'

'Well, we've kept in touch and we meet up occasionally. He's now working for MI5 or something similar. It's all hush-hush, of course. I can give you his home phone number and you could give him a ring. It's quite possible he might be able to point you in the right direction to get it sorted out.'

She studied me for a few seconds, waiting for my reaction. Then she added, 'That's if you want to, of course.'

'I don't really know what Lena wants to do,' I replied thoughtfully. 'But it sounds like a good idea. Yes, I would like his number.'

It was at this instant that Lena appeared in the kitchen. She was dressed in a skirt and a blouse. They were slightly too big for her, but the transformation from the drab kaftan I had seen her wearing at Boris's house to this simple outfit was outstanding. She had brushed her hair and she looked exceedingly pretty. She carried a pair of shoes in her hand.

'They are too big,' she announced, looking first at the shoes, then at Pippa, and then at me. 'They keep falling off. I will have to make them smaller.'

'We'll sort something out,' I assured her.

The reaction from Pippa was to make a face and demand, 'Where's that coffee?'

Lena reacted quickly. 'I will make it.'

Five minutes later we were sitting round the table, each sipping a mug of coffee and chatting – or rather Pippa and I did most of the talking and Lena listened, though clearly taking an active interest.

At last Pippa announced that she had work to do and got up to leave. As she walked towards the kitchen door Lena uttered a rather shy 'Thank you'.

Pippa looked over her shoulder and smiled. 'You're welcome.'

I followed her to the front door. She turned to face me. I immediately gave her a hug. 'A million thanks for your help. I'll make it up to you.'

She grinned. 'I'll make sure you do.'

As she walked down the path I called after her. 'About Patrick – if you can give me his phone number I would appreciate having it.'

'Will do!' Pippa shouted back, already getting into her car.

The car door slammed, the engine roared into life and with a wave of her hand Pippa departed.

I returned to the kitchen, where Lena was still sitting. She was holding the shoes again and looking at them intently, clearly thinking about how to make them serviceable.

Guessing her thought pattern, I came to the rescue. I found some cardboard and we cut out several inner soles to pack them out. When we had finished, at least she could wear them, though they were still a bit big for her.

Lena was very quiet the whole time, but she brightened up when I announced, 'Now we'll go and buy you some proper clothes to wear.'

She disappeared upstairs to get ready while I glanced at my mail, which had just arrived.

I had only got through the first couple of envelopes when she reappeared. She was now wearing a short jacket, which Pippa must also have provided. This solved another problem for me, because though the sun was shining the day was still cool and I had been concerned whether she would be warm enough while we were out.

We made our way to the shops. Once there, Lena knew what she wanted. She darted from shop to shop accumulating a wardrobe. Each time she saw something she liked she would hold it up and look at me as if seeking my approval as well as my permission to have it. I would give my opinion by a nod or a shake of the head. I obligingly paid for each purchase with my credit card.

After about an hour she had acquired quite a practical wardrobe. A skirt, two blouses and a pair of slacks were followed by a pair of jeans. Next, it was the underwear section of a large department store that took Lena's attention. She would hold up each flimsy garment and look to me shyly for approval. Most of the items she selected were of a skimpy nature. Everything she bought in that department seemed to fit into quite a small bag. Just as we were about to leave the store, Lena spotted the cosmetic counter. Here she seemed again to know what she wanted, and several more items were added to the bags we carried. By now the money I was spending was adding up considerably.

The last item on Lena's agenda was a pair of shoes, to replace the ones she was wearing. I observed that in spite of our earlier modifications, they threatened to slip off with every step she took. Buying the shoes was a protracted process, as Lena tried on one pair after another. In the end, practicality prevailed and she purchased a pair of soft leather flat ones.

At last it seemed that she was satisfied with all her purchases. As we left the shoe shop, she turned to me with a cheerful smile. 'Thank you. I will pay you back as soon as I can. Please tell me how much I need to pay you.'

I smiled and nodded. It had been my pleasure. Somehow I did not mind whether Lena paid me back or not. It was now long past midday. I asked her if she was hungry, and her enthusiastic smile and nod of the head prompted me to lead the way to a pub where I knew we could get a meal.

Over the next hour we sampled a ploughman's lunch from the pub menu. I indulged in my usual half-pint of lager, while Lena wanted to know what cider was. In the end she decided to try a half-pint of draught cider and appeared to approve of its taste. Over the meal our conversation was of a relaxed nature as we tried to get used to each other's company.

The afternoon was well advanced when we at last made our way home. We each carried several bags, but on the way Lena suddenly transferred her load to one hand and with the other took my free hand. It was a pleasant feeling.

Back home I had several jobs to attend to. Lena had already disappeared with all the purchases, after asking if she could put them in the wardrobe in the bedroom.

It was early evening by the time she reappeared. Now she was dressed in the new skirt and one of the blouses we had purchased. For the first time, I saw her wearing lipstick, and there was a faint hint of perfume about her.

'How do I look?' she asked, as she modelled her outfit in front of me.

'You look great,' I enthused.

Her reaction was immediate. Suddenly she moved towards me and planted a kiss on my cheek. 'Thank you,' she whispered.

I suddenly had the inclination to take her in my arms, but her spontaneous act had been brief. The next instant she moved back and asked, 'What can I make for supper?'

Together we went into the kitchen and investigated the contents of my fridge and cupboards. Lena spied some cheese and suggested that it needed using up. The result was that we sat down to cheese on toast. I was growing quite impressed with her handling of everything.

We chatted for a while. I was anxious to learn more about her and how she came to be with Boris, but though she seemed happy to talk about more mundane things, she appeared to be guarded about her background. The situation still puzzled me, but I decided to put any further prompting on hold for a while. Perhaps in time Lena would open up and tell me what I wanted to know.

The evening passed quickly. Eventually Lena asked me, almost shyly, if it would be all right if she went upstairs. I readily assented, and she quickly disappeared. I remained where I was, reading the newspaper, which had been delivered as usual that morning but I had had no time to read.

I could hear Lena in the bathroom upstairs, and at last all went quiet. After turning out the downstairs lights, I quietly made my way upstairs. The bedroom door was open and Lena was tucked up in bed. There was a faint smell of perfume in the air, which I found very agreeable.

I spent ten minutes or so in the bathroom and then I was ready to join her. It suddenly occurred to me that during our shopping spree we had not purchased any nightclothes for her. I guessed she would make do with the pyjamas I had provided.

She appeared to be asleep as I crept into bed, but I was wrong. As I made myself comfortable she turned towards me and snuggled up to me, her lips finding mine. When we came into contact with each other, I realised that she was not wearing the pyjamas.

Chapter 6

Over the next few days Lena and I settled down to domestic bliss, such as it was – an open-ended arrangement, as I was still not completely clear what her intentions were; but on the second day of our relationship she asked me if she could stay a little longer with me.

'Of course you can,' I replied, kissing her.

Her response was a sweet smile, a return kiss and the words 'Thank you'.

The truth was that now I was becoming more and more attracted to her and I enjoyed having her around. As I worked at home most of the time, I had ample opportunity to study her.

Every morning she would get up first and prepare our breakfast. We would eat together, and then I would retreat to my den to write and making telephone calls. Mid-morning, she would tap at my door and shyly put a mug of coffee on my desk. After lunch we would spend the afternoon pottering about. She had completely taken over all the domestic chores and appeared to enjoy doing them, taking delight in providing meals for us both and doing various jobs around the house. Our relationship had been strengthened by the unexpected physical contact on her second night's stay. When this was repeated, I realised that the chemistry between us was changing. Slowly I found myself falling in love with her.

I was still puzzled about her background, however. She talked very little about her past and her life in Germany before Boris had obviously persuaded her to come to England with him. When I questioned her, she seemed to be wary and her answers told me very little. She said that her mother lived in Poland, and that she had worked for an American company in West Berlin, but that was about as much as I could glean from her.

On the second day of Lena's stay, Pippa kept her promise to give me Patrick's telephone number. I had just settled down to do some work in my den after breakfast when she rang me. For once she was up quite early, though I soon learned that there was a reason for this: she was going away.

While we were chatting I was conscious of a conversation taking place in the kitchen. To my concern, I remembered that this was one of the days Mrs Batty came in and I had not alerted Lena to this. I need not have worried, as when I had finished with the telephone call to Pippa I hurried to the kitchen and discovered that they were getting on like a house on fire – so much so that Mrs Batty, on observing Lena walking about without shoes, decided to go back to her house to fetch a pair of slippers for her, muttering as she passed me in the hall, 'Catch herself a death of cold, going about like that.' She returned five minutes later with a pair of what looked like new slippers, which apparently her daughter had been given and refused to wear. Lena seemed quite pleased with them, though she did seem to be just as happy pottering about the house barefoot.

Still concerned about Lena's illegal status, that evening I telephoned Patrick. I was unsuccessful on the first occasion. However, the second time I tried I managed to speak to him. His immediate response was guarded, but when I explained that Pippa had given me his telephone number and he realised who I was he seemed to relax and be pleased to talk to me.

I waited until the greetings and small talk had finished before I brought up the object of my call. 'Pippa thinks you may be able to help me.'

'In what way?'

I hesitated before answering, but I realised that I would have to be frank with Patrick in order to obtain any help. 'I have a young lady staying with me who is apparently in the country illegally. I was wondering if you could advise me of the best way to rectify things, or perhaps point me in the right direction to find out more.'

Patrick's reply was slow and calculated. 'Hmm. It's a bit outside of my field of expertise, but I may be able to put you in touch with somebody.'

'That would be a great help,' I replied.

'Fine. Pleased to be of assistance.' He paused for a second. 'Look, why don't we meet up for lunch? It would be nice to catch up.'

'I'd enjoy that.'

'Do you come to London at all?'

'That's no problem,' I replied eagerly.

'Do you know the Dog and Duck in Soho?'

'I can find it. I think I know the place.'

'How about tomorrow – say, around twelve?'

'I'll be there.'

'Great. See you then.'

I put the phone down, pleased with my efforts. I had made some progress on a problem that had been bothering me ever since Lena had come to stay. While I still did not know what her intentions were, it would be nice to know what the situation was regarding her status in Britain. I had no intention at this stage of discussing this matter with her. I felt it best to be in possession of the right answer first.

The next day I made my way up to London after telling Lena I would be out for several hours. It was just coming up to midday when I found the Dog and Duck. I ventured inside to find Patrick already sitting at a table in a secluded corner. He rose to greet me, full of smiles. Though I had not seen him for several years, I recognised him immediately by his mop of red hair.

We chatted about old times for several minutes, at the same time studying the food menu. Patrick declared that he would have the cottage pie, remarking that it was a good choice he had enjoyed previously. I opted to join him. I would have gone to the bar to order, but he insisted that he would do the honours and enquired what I would like to drink. I requested my usual half-pint of lager.

While we were waiting for the food and sipping our drinks, Patrick brought up a more serious matter. 'I understand you have a bit of a problem.'

I nodded. 'Yes, I would like to get some facts on how to proceed if necessary.'

'Fire away.'

'I'd better start at the beginning,' I replied. I thought for a few seconds. 'Do you remember Boris Smirnov, who was at university at the same time as us?'

Patrick nodded. 'Yes, I do. In fact, he works for the same organisation as I do, only in another department.'

'Gosh, that's interesting. What a coincidence!'

Patrick smiled. 'Yes, it is. But tell me more about your problem.'

Carefully I explained what had happened since my chance encounter with Boris in Soho. I was interrupted halfway through by the arrival of our meal. While I was talking Patrick listened, his face showing no particular emotion.

When I had finished, he turned his attention to his cottage pie. After a minute or two he looked up at me. 'But you say that the lady in question hasn't indicated that she wants to stay in this country.'

'That's correct.'

Patrick studied me for a second. 'Do you think she wants to stay with you?' he asked.

'I'm not sure,' I admitted.

There was a few seconds' silence, as we both attended to our food.

Suddenly Patrick looked at me again. 'What's the lady's name?' he asked.

I was surprised at the question, but I quickly replied, 'Lena – Lena Bergmann.'

Patrick seemed surprised. 'Lena Bergmann?'

'Yes.'

He looked at me but made no reply.

'Do you think you might be able to provide me with some information?' I asked.

'Of course. But I need to find out more from a colleague. I'll have to come back to you.'

'That would be fine.'

'Does Lena know you're meeting me?' he asked, almost casually.

I shook my head. 'No. I thought I should get some information first.'

Patrick nodded. 'That'll be the best thing. Leave it with me.'

For the rest of the meal we chatted about other things, mostly our university days, recalling various events, Pippa and other students we both knew. Eventually Patrick glanced at his watch and said that he had to leave.

'Give me a day or so and I'll be in touch,' he announced, as we shook hands and parted.

I made my way to the tube. I was pleased with my efforts so far and it had been pleasant to meet up with Patrick again.

It was close to mid-afternoon when I reached home. Lena was in the kitchen, but as I entered the hall she came out full of smiles and planted a kiss on my cheek. She was wearing one of the new blouses and the skirt I had bought for her. I thought she looked very attractive – so different from the Lena I had first encountered at Boris's house.

'Did you have a nice time in London?' she asked breezily.

I nodded. 'Yes, I did. I met up with an old friend I knew at university.'

'Would you like a cup of coffee?' Lena asked. She smiled. 'I was just going to make one for myself.'

'That would be great,' I replied with a grin.

I followed her into the kitchen and sat at the table while she busied herself. It did not take long before a mug was placed in front of me. Lena sat opposite me, her hands clasped round her coffee, looking at me intently. She was the first to speak.

'We need to buy some more coffee, and the milk is almost gone.'

Before I could answer she spoke again. 'There is a shop at the end of the road. I could get some there and there is also a hairdresser there. I would like to go there.' She tugged at her hair as she spoke.

'That sounds like a good idea,' I agreed.

Lena sipped her coffee. She looked at me coyly. 'But I will need more money.'

'Don't worry. I'll give you some,' I assured her with a smile.

'I will pay you back for the hairdresser,' she replied hurriedly.

From our conversation it seemed as if Lena might have already ventured out, although I pondered the thought that Mrs Batty might have told her about the shop and the hairdresser. Mrs Batty appeared to have quite taken to her, spending time chatting to her and taking a delight in explaining various things. I think perhaps she found Lena easier to advise than her own two daughters.

At that instant the telephone rang. I had intended to lead the conversation on to the subject of Lena's stay with me. She was quite different in demeanour from when she had first arrived and now was attentive and loving towards me. Yet I had to admit that I still knew very little about her. She was a mystery, and I was intrigued.

I answered the telephone, hoping that it might be Patrick calling, but it was someone trying to sell something. When I returned to the kitchen Lena was busy writing on a bit of paper. She looked up.

'I owe you a lot of money. I will give it to you when I go back to Germany,' she announced.

It was the opportunity I had been waiting for. 'Are you going back?' I asked softly.

Lena looked at me questioningly. 'Can I stay a little longer? I like being here.'

It was the answer I wanted. I moved over to her, and taking hold of her hands I planted a kiss on her lips. 'Of course you can. I like having you around.'

'Thank you,' she whispered.

I gave her some money and she went off cheerfully to the shops at the end of the road. When she came back she had visited the hairdresser and seemed quite pleased with the result. Her fair hair now fell to her shoulders, gleaming in the light. She had clearly had the full works, because the nails on both her hands and her feet were now painted a delicate pink.

When I appeared she greeted me with a smile. 'How do I look?'

'Stunning,' I replied, putting my arms around her and kissing her.

Eventually she wriggled away from me. She glanced down at the bag she was carrying. 'I bought a cake in the shop,' she announced. 'Can we have a slice of it and a cup of coffee?' she asked wistfully.

I laughed. 'Of course we can, but remember it will make you fat,' I warned jokingly.

Lena made a face. 'I know, but I do not eat cake very often.' She added, 'I will keep slim for you.'

It was only the day before that I had told Lena she had a nice slim figure. It was quite true. She had a very good figure. I was also intrigued by the fact that on most nights she slept naked. As I had always slept practically naked, we tended to match each other.

Lena's lack of sleeping attire revealed another mystery about her. One morning I woke up very early, before she had carried out her usual routine of disappearing first. It was already light, and she was sleeping with one arm on top of the covers. It was then for the first time that I noticed a small tattoo high up on her arm. It was an ornamental letter of the alphabet – it looked like an A surrounded by a circle. It intrigued me and I wondered what the story was behind it.

When I broached the subject at breakfast, Lena blushed slightly and just replied quietly, 'It was done a long time ago.'

I sensed that she did not want to elaborate, so I left it at that. It was another mysterious piece of her background.

The following evening Patrick telephoned. 'I need to see you again, urgently,' was his first statement.

'Of course,' I agreed. 'When?'

'Can you make it tomorrow?'

'Yes. I'm free. Where, and what time?'

'Can you get to London for eleven?'

'Yes, I can. Same place?'

'No. They won't be open. There's a coffee bar almost next door. I'll be there.'

'That's fine. I look forward to seeing you.'

There was no further conversation between us. We said goodbye and that was that.

I wondered what information Patrick had for me. I hoped it would be positive and helpful. I did not relish the thought of being parted from Lena now. There had to be a way of enabling her to stay with me legally. That thought made me all the more eager to find out what Patrick had to say.

Chapter 7

It was a bright sunny morning when I set out for London and my meeting with Patrick. I was glad I had allowed myself plenty of time to get to my destination, because the train was twenty minutes late. It was just coming up to eleven when I entered the street where the Dog and Duck was situated.

From Patrick's brief description I had expected to find one of those small coffee bars that abound in London, but I was wrong. The only place resembling a coffee bar that was almost next to the pub proved to be a much larger establishment with tables one could sit at and have a meal. I was still not sure if I had found the right place as I entered. However, I was correct. Almost immediately I spied Patrick sitting at a table, a cup in front of him.

He jumped up to greet me as I approached, and held out his hand. 'Hello again. Can I get you a coffee or tea?'

'Hello. Coffee would be nice. Just black.'

Patrick nodded and hurried over to the counter. A few minutes later he returned with my coffee and sat down again. 'Nice morning.' He nodded in the direction of the bright sunny street outside.

'Yes,' I replied. I was eager to hear what, if any, information he had for me. I steered the conversation to the matter in hand. 'Did you manage to find out anything?' I asked.

Patrick looked at me intently. There was a pause before he answered. When he did, it was with slow and carefully chosen

51

words. 'Yes, I have, but I'm not sure if it's the information you would wish to hear.'

I was immediately alert, anxious to hear more. The tone of Patrick's voice was not encouraging. What did he mean by something I might not wish to hear?

'What have you found out? Tell me,' I urged, now concerned about what his reply was going to be.

Patrick took his time in answering, as if formulating what he wanted to say. 'I must stress that what I'm going to tell you is highly confidential. I'm breaking every rule in the book, but I think you should know and I respect you to keep what I'm going to say to yourself.'

'Of course.' I was now extremely anxious to learn what was so confidential. I waited for Patrick to tell me more.

He was still studying me closely as he spoke again. 'The fact is that Lena Bergmann is wanted for questioning by both the American and the Russian security services.'

The information hit me like a bolt from the blue. 'You're joking,' I managed to respond.

Patrick shook his head. 'I'm afraid not,' he replied, looking quite grave.

'But… but what is she supposed to have done?' I stammered.

'She is accused of spying against both countries.'

'WHAT?' I struggled to absorb what Patrick had just said. It all sounded too ridiculous.

'But that's impossible,' I protested. 'There must be a mistake. Are you sure we're talking about the same person?'

Patrick shook his head. 'I'm sorry, but it's correct. My delay in coming back to you was to ensure that we had the right person.'

'But how and when is all this supposed to have happened?'

'It's a long story,' he replied, taking a sip of coffee.

I was quiet for a short time. What Patrick had just told me seemed ludicrous. I found it impossible to imagine the gentle Lena involved in some sort of spying escapade.

'Lena doesn't look to me like the type to be involved in cloak-and-dagger stuff,' I remarked.

Patrick started to lift his cup again, but at my comment he suddenly put it down. He paused, to ensure my full attention. His voice was firm and calm. 'Look, I know you may perhaps have an attraction to this woman, but you have to accept the facts. This information comes from the highest authority.'

'But she's such a kind and loving person,' I protested.

Patrick shook his head. 'That's a strategy these people use. That's how they get information.'

'How do you mean?'

Patrick smiled briefly. 'Lena is a double agent. She visits East Germany from time to time. Putting it bluntly, she gets to know some individual high up there, sleeps with him, extracts information from him and then travels back and relates it to the Americans. The problem is that she also does the same thing in return. Sleeps with an American, gets secret information out of him and then transfers that back to the Russians.'

'It all sounds almost unbelievable.'

Patrick nodded. 'Yes, indeed. But that's the way things work in these circles. It's been done many times before. Ours can be a pretty lousy business.'

I was silent for a minute, trying to take in what I had just learnt. It still seemed incredible that Lena could be involved in such a thing, but Patrick was sure of his facts. After all, I reasoned, that was his job. I recalled how sweet Lena had been to me. Was it all fake? When we had made love on her second night at my house, was that part of some kind of deception? But why was she doing it to me? I had no secrets to divulge. It all seemed unreal. More to the point, what was I to do about it?

Patrick broke me out of my musing. 'Tim, I have to ask you again to keep this confidential.'

I nodded. 'OK,' I replied. 'But what about Lena? What happens to her now?'

Patrick's answer came quickly. 'Her case is being taken up by another department, by someone higher up than me. A decision will be made shortly. She might have to go back to Germany.'

'You mean, be arrested?'

'Yes. That's on the cards.'

'And in the meantime?'

Patrick shrugged. 'Just carry on as normal. Say nothing to Lena about our conversation. I'll contact you again as soon as I know more.'

So it looked as if everything was all being planned out. I was not an important player in the game.

I suddenly thought of something else. 'How does Boris Smirnov fit into all this?' I asked.

'I'll go into that in more detail later.' Patrick glanced at his watch. 'Sorry, Tim. If you're OK with everything, I have to go.' He took a last swig of his coffee.

'Yes, of course,' I asserted.

Just as he was about to leave, Patrick reached into his pocket, pulled out a card and then scribbled something on it. He handed it to me. 'If you want to contact me urgently, use this number.' He added, almost as an afterthought, 'You'd better choose a code word.'

'Anything?' I asked.

'Anything.'

I hurriedly looked around the café. It had a distinct Italian flavour. Posters depicting Italian scenes decorated the walls. My eyes fixed on one, a picture of Sorrento.

'Sorrento,' I replied.

'Sorrento it is.'

Our parting was quick and hurried. I remained at the table, finishing my coffee and trying to make sense of what I had just heard. It all seemed so unreal – fiction rather than fact. It almost seemed as if I were living in the plot of one of my novels.

I left the coffee bar and visited several bookshops I knew, but somehow browsing the shelves didn't work. The events of the morning were still very much uppermost in my mind.

Eventually I made my way home. It was early afternoon when I reached my front door. I was surprised to find the house empty. I wondered where Lena could be, and then assumed that she had gone shopping for food. After all, I reasoned, she was not a prisoner and was free to go where she pleased. I recalled that she would still have money available to spend, because on the last occasion she had asked for some, I had given her far more than the value of the goods she was going to buy.

I wandered into my den, carrying the post that had arrived. Several letters required some action, and the next hour passed very quickly. I had just about finished the mundane jobs, still musing over the events of the morning, when the noise of the front door opening alerted me to Lena's return. I went into the hall to greet her. She was carrying several bags.

Her face lit up as I appeared. Immediately she placed a kiss on my cheek. 'Hello, darling. Did you have a nice time in London?' She had a charming accent.

I put my arm around her and returned her kiss. 'I did indeed,' I replied.

She broke free from me and laughed. 'Now you have lipstick on your face,' she giggled, rummaging in her bag for a tissue. Then, still filled with excitement, she turned her attention to one of the bags she was carrying. 'I went to the shops and there was this street with lots of stalls selling things. I bought this from one of them…' She pulled out a dress and held it up in front of her. 'What do you think?'

'It looks fine, but I'd like to see you wearing it,' I replied. I had not seen her in a dress, and the germ of an idea was coming into my thoughts.

'I will put it on soon for you,' she replied. Her hand dived into the bag once more. She was clearly excited. 'I bought these as well in the market.'

She held up a pair of sandals and then dropped them onto the floor. The next moment she was slipping her feet into them. 'What do you think?' she asked again.

The sandals were brief in the extreme, having only a few slim straps to hold them on. They showed off her newly painted toenails to good advantage.

'They look great, and they'll go well with the dress,' I replied, smiling.

She looked at me rather coyly. 'I owe you more money now.'

I smiled again. 'That's all right. Make it a present from me.' I put my arms around her, and once again we kissed.

Suddenly she pulled back and looked at me. 'Have you had anything to eat?' she asked.

I shook my head. 'No. Nothing since breakfast.'

'I am starving. I will make us some food,' she announced.

I followed her into the kitchen.

Lena opened the door of the fridge, looked into it and then quickly shut the door again. Next she turned her attention to the food cupboard. She spied a tin of baked beans on the shelf and quickly grabbed it. Holding it up, she turned to me. 'How about beans on toast?' she asked, with a questioning look.

'That would be great,' I replied, with a smile.

Tin opener in hand, she suddenly wailed, 'Oh, no! I forgot to get something to eat for tonight.' She stopped what she was doing and looked at me. 'I will go to the shop—'

I laughed. My germ of an idea was coming to fruition. 'Don't worry,' I interjected. 'I'll take you out to dinner.'

Lena looked at me enquiringly. The next moment, she planted another kiss on my cheek. 'Thank you,' she whispered.

It was midway through the evening when we left the house. Lena had spent some time getting ready, and when she at last appeared coming down the stairs, I was amazed at how she looked. She was wearing the new dress, a white summer one with tie straps that left her shoulders and arms bare. The sandals completed her outfit. She looked extremely pretty and I felt proud to be taking her out. As we left the house, she slipped her hand into mine.

I felt that we must look like an engaged couple as we walked along the street. At the same time, I wondered if I was really walking with an alleged spy. Was everything all pretend? I brushed aside the thought. It was something I would deal with later.

We did not have far to go. There was a pub in the next road that served food and had a good reputation. Fortunately it was not crowded and we had a nice table in a corner. Lena asked for fish with new potatoes, and after studying the menu I opted for the same. A bottle of house wine proved to be an excellent accompaniment.

During the meal I tried to prise more information from Lena. Following Patrick's revelation I was anxious to learn more about her – to find out more about her background. My efforts produced a limited result. Lena told me that she had spent her childhood in Poland. Then her father had been killed and her mother had married a Russian and the family had gone to live in East Germany. Now Lena lived in Berlin, where she had been working for a large American engineering company. She had an apartment not far from her place of work. Her mother had returned to Poland after parting from her second husband. I tried to establish how Lena had been persuaded by Boris to come to England, but her answers were vague. It seemed that there was still a mystery surrounding her. I thought again about what Patrick had told me earlier, but I still found it hard to comprehend that the pretty girl dining with me was a spy.

The conversation was by no means one-sided. Lena wanted to know about my family, whether my parents were still alive, and how I had become a writer. I answered all her questions as honestly as I could.

We took a long time over our meal and it was late when we left the pub. As we walked home Lena slipped her arm through mine. It was quite a warm evening for April, with a clear sky and the moon just beginning to appear. It would have been a perfect evening but for the questions hanging over Lena.

Once back at my house, we went into the kitchen and Lena made us each a mug of cocoa. We took quite a time sipping it slowly. At last, with a glance at the clock on the wall, Lena announced that she was going to the bathroom. For the next ten minutes I busied myself washing up the mugs and pottering about in the kitchen.

After a while all went quiet upstairs and I made my way to the bathroom. Five minutes later I crept into the bedroom draped in a towel. There was perfume in the air. A figure emerged from the gloom. Lena put her arms around me and pressed her lips to mine. I could feel that she was wearing little or no clothing. The towel was pulled away from me and we stumbled towards the bed, still in each other's arms.

For the next four days I waited to hear from Patrick, but he did not contact me. In the meantime I was still enjoying having Lena around. She had not made any further mention of returning to Germany, for which I was glad. For most of the time, we acted like a newly married couple. For me, only one thing marred our relationship, and that was the uncertainty and the questions that were hanging over her. I had grown quite fond of her and I still found it difficult to accept the description of her given to me by Patrick. It seemed to me that if she was faking everything about our relationship, she was making a superb job of it. One thing was clear: until I heard from Patrick again, all I could do was wait.

When something did happen, it was sudden and completely out of the blue. On that particular morning, the frequent times I had given money to Lena for shopping meant that I had to replenish my supply of cash. A visit to the bank was necessary.

I left Lena happily waiting for the arrival of Mrs Batty. Mrs Batty had taken a definite motherly interest in her, advising her about this and that, and muttering to me things like, 'Poor girl. Away from all her friends and family.' Where she thought I fitted into the picture, I had no idea.

I was not long at the bank and I returned hurriedly to the house, just beating the rain that had been threatening to fall all morning. As I let myself into the hall, I was met by a distraught Mrs Batty. Hardly giving me time to close the front door, she burst out, 'Oh, Mr Mallon, it's Lena. They've took her away.'

Chapter 8

When I saw Mrs Batty looking so distressed, it took me several seconds to quite adjust to the situation. 'What happened?' I asked anxiously, already expecting the worst.

All she could manage was, 'Lena. Took her away, they did.'

I knew I had to calm her down before I could get a grasp of what had happened. I took control. Trying to appear calm myself, I took her arm and gently led her into the kitchen, at the same time saying quietly, 'Come and sit down and tell me about it.' She obediently complied, and we sat down at the kitchen table.

'Now, tell me what happened.'

Mrs Batty took a deep breath. 'It was just after you left. The doorbell rang and I went to answer it. There was a man and a woman there, and a big black car on the drive with another man in it.' She paused.

'What did they say?' I urged.

'They just said, "We want to see…" I can't remember the name they said. It was something like Birdman.'

'Bergmann?' I suggested.

'Yes, that was it – Bergmann.'

'What happened then?' I asked gently.

'Well, Lena heard the commotion and came to see what was going on. And… and then they just said to her, "You're coming with us."' She paused again.

'And then?' I prompted.

'Just grabbed her, they did, and… and she's struggling with them and saying, "No, no!" all the time.'

Mrs Batty hesitated again and then continued. 'Took her they did, put handcuffs on her, and forced her into the car. Took her just like that, no shoes on her feet, and no coat.'

'Did they say who they were?' I asked, trying to appear as calm as possible.

She gave me a surprised look. 'Why? It must have been the police.'

I did not share Mrs Batty's assumption. It did not sound like the British police. Even at their worst, that was not how they acted.

'But what's she done, Mr Mallon, to be treated like that?' Mrs Batty asked.

'I don't know,' I replied.

'But what are we going to do?' she wailed.

I was thinking desperately. I wished I had been here when the incident happened, but now the prime issue was to find out what had actually taken place – and, more importantly, where Lena was. My immediate thought was that she had indeed been arrested, as Patrick had warned me. I toyed with the idea of contacting the police, but on second thoughts that did not seem to be the right thing to do. It suddenly came to me loud and clear: contact Patrick.

Mrs Batty was still looking at me, clearly expecting a reply. I knew I had to show some sort of control.

'I'll have to make some telephone calls,' I announced, sounding as positive as I could. Quickly I thought of something else to occupy Mrs Batty in the meantime. 'Look, why don't you make us both some tea while I do that?'

The suggestion worked. She immediately set about the task. I hurried to my den, the main thing on my mind to get in touch with Patrick. I thanked my lucky stars that I had a telephone number to contact him.

The telephone seemed to ring for a long time, but I hung on for several minutes. Then a woman's voice answered with what sounded like the name of a company, but it was not clear or understandable.

'I want to talk to Patrick Jenson,' I announced.

'Please give me the address you are calling from.'

I was a bit thrown, but I complied with the request.

'And the telephone number,' the voice continued.

Again I gave details.

'Do you have a code word?'

'Yes.'

'Please give it to me.'

'Sorrento.'

'Please wait.'

There was another long pause, and then the voice came again, impersonal and precise. 'The person you are calling will contact you.'

The line went dead.

I replaced the receiver. I was puzzled and slightly irritated by the response I had received. In my ignorance I had expected the telephone to be answered by Patrick, or at least that I would be put through to him. I kicked myself for not advising the mechanical voice that my call was of an urgent nature. Now all I could do was wait.

I returned to the kitchen. Mrs Batty was busy with the teapot, but when I entered she looked at me, her expression seeking information.

'I've telephoned a friend who knows about these things. He's going to come back to me. I'm sure it can all be sorted out,' I announced, hoping that I sounded more confident than I felt.

Mrs Batty looked a bit puzzled but appeared to accept my explanation. She handed me a mug of tea.

After spending five minutes with Mrs Batty over the tea, I returned to my den. There was some work waiting for me, but somehow I felt unable to settle down to it. An hour passed. I wondered if I should telephone the number again, but in the end I decided not to. Mrs Batty left, still concerned about Lena. I assured her that as soon as I knew something I would let her know.

Just after she departed the telephone rang. I quickly picked it up and answered. A familiar voice spoke. 'Patrick. You wanted me.'

I plunged straight in. 'Patrick, what's happening and where is Lena? What's going on?'

'Sorry, I don't follow. What's happened?'

'Lena appears to have either been arrested or abducted by somebody.'

'Tell me more.' Patrick was calm but brusque.

'I was out at the time, but my understanding is that two men and a woman arrived and took Lena away with them by force.'

'When did this happen?'

'Around half past ten, I think.'

'Were they in plain clothes?'

'Yes, I believe so.'

'Any other details?'

'No, I'm afraid not. It was my cleaner who witnessed it all.'

'Hmm. Leave this with me.'

'What about the police? Should they be informed?' To me it seemed a logical thing to do.

'Leave all that to me. I'll sort it out. In the meantime stay near the phone. I'll come back to you. Goodbye for now.'

I hardly had time to utter a quick 'OK' before there was a click and the line went dead. Once again I would have to wait.

Hours passed. By mid-afternoon I realised that I needed to eat something, having had nothing since breakfast. I wandered into the kitchen. With no inclination to cook a big meal, in the end I boiled myself a couple of eggs and made a pot of tea.

I was halfway through my spartan meal when the telephone rang again. I hastened to answer it. It wasn't Patrick. It was my agent, who wanted to clarify something. Though the call was important, I felt concerned that my telephone was occupied for ten minutes or so.

I returned to the kitchen and poured myself another mug of tea. I had hardly finished this task when the telephone rang again. Once again I hurried to answer it.

Patrick announced himself.

I jumped in straight away. 'What's happened? Do you know where Lena is?'

'I have some limited information,' he replied.

'Tell me,' I urged, desperate to know more.

Patrick appeared to hesitate for a few seconds before making a reply. When he did it was with a well-thought-out sentence. 'I think we can safely assume that Lena is now on the way back to Berlin.'

'But how? Who's behind this?' I demanded.

'Information is a bit vague at this stage, but I think you can be confident that what I have just told you is correct.'

'But what happens now?' I protested. 'She's been kidnapped.'

'On the surface, it would appear that way.'

'But can't anything be done?' I persisted. 'Surely we can get on to the authorities in Germany and demand to know what's going on?'

Patrick had a ready reply. 'We have to remember that she is not a British citizen. We cannot make demands on another country unless there is a good reason to do so.'

'But she was living with me and has been abducted from my house.'

'Yes. But don't forget she was staying in the country illegally.'

'I know, but surely something can be done,' I argued. Somehow I felt that Patrick had more information that he was not going to share with me. As I was a major participant in the whole affair, it seemed a bit odd.

'We'll just have to wait and see what happens,' he replied. 'As soon as I hear anything, I will let you know.'

'But you intimated that Lena faced arrest if she was returned to Germany.'

'That could still happen. It depends on who is holding her.'

Desperation began to overtake me. 'That seems a bit unfair,' I retorted.

Patrick was quick to respond. 'Look, Tim, I know that you have most likely got quite fond of the girl, but you have to accept the fact that she is a dangerous person to get involved with. I tried to explain that to you a few days ago.'

It took me several seconds to think up a suitable reply. In the meantime, Patrick spoke again.

'Leave things with me. As I said, as soon as I know more, I will contact you again.'

Disappointed as I was, my reply was brief. 'Very well.'

'I'm afraid I'll have to ring off now. I expect I don't have to remind you that everything we have talked about is still confidential.'

'Of course,' I replied.

Our goodbyes were short and sharp, and I put the phone down grappling to come to terms with everything that had happened during the last few hours. It all seemed unreal. Despite what Patrick had told me, I still could not fully think of Lena as the kind of person he described. If what he said was true, then she was an excellent actress. But why would she pick on me? I had no secrets to reveal during moments of passion. I recalled the previous night and the person who had embraced me so lovingly. Was I to believe that this had all been made up? Somehow I found it difficult to believe all of Patrick's story.

I wandered back into the kitchen and almost in a dream I washed up the few things I had used. The house seemed unusually quiet. I picked up the newspaper, which had been lying on the hall table all day, but I could not concentrate on reading it.

Towards the evening Mrs Batty popped in to see if I had any information about Lena. I explained to her that Lena had had to return to Germany and that I was waiting to hear more details. I wasn't sure whether she really believed me, but it was the best I could do in the circumstances. Even conveying this information to her made me wonder if I had actually broken the promise of confidentiality I had given Patrick.

The evening passed slowly. I had a faint hope that I would receive another call from Patrick, but none came. In the end I turned in at around half past ten. Even doing this brought back memories of Lena: a faint reminder of her perfume remained in the bedroom, and items of her clothing were in view.

After a rather disturbed night, I woke up late. The sound of the newspaper being pushed through the letterbox alerted me to the time. I got up slowly and eventually made my way into the kitchen for breakfast. I turned the radio on for company, my usual routine prior to Lena's arrival.

After breakfast I wandered into my den and tried to do some work, but I found it impossible to concentrate. Twice the telephone rang, but each time my hope that Patrick would be on the other end of the line was clouded with disappointment.

The day passed slowly, as did the next, and still there was no communication from Patrick. Almost sick with worry, on the evening of the second day I could wait no longer. I decided to call him at his home. The telephone rang for a long time and I was just about to put it down when he answered.

'It's Tim here,' I began. 'I wondered if you had any further news for me.' I did not let my voice indicate the disappointment I had being experiencing at not hearing anything earlier.

'Hello, Tim. Sorry I was so long getting to the phone. I was answering the front door. I was going to ring you this evening.'

'You have more information?' I asked hopefully.

'In a sense, yes. I learned today that Lena is in East Berlin.'

'What? But that's the communist side!' I exclaimed.

'Correct. Lena travels there quite a lot.'

'But who's abducted her? Has she been arrested?' I pressed him for more information, hoping that I would not hear the worst news.

'It doesn't seem so. She appears to be a free woman, from the reports coming in.'

'But that's crazy,' I protested. 'Why was she abducted from my doorstep?'

'Hmm. Difficult one.' Patrick paused for a moment. Then, 'I suppose your cleaning lady's account of what happened is accurate?'

'I think so,' I replied.

'Sometimes in situations like that people can embellish the facts.'

'I suppose so,' I responded gloomily. Even as I uttered the words, I was not convinced that Mrs Batty's description of events had in any way been exaggerated. I returned to the issue. 'But even so, Lena was clearly taken by force,' I pointed out.

I was not expecting Patrick's next remark. 'It could have been a hoax,' he suggested.

'Nonsense,' I retorted. 'You don't go to all that trouble... And for what reason?'

'Well, we'll just have to wait and see what happens.'

'I suppose so,' I conceded. It didn't seem as if I was going to get anything more out of Patrick.

Perhaps he detected something in the tone of my voice, because he immediately responded with the assurance, 'If anything more comes through that is relevant to you, I'll contact you.'

'Please do,' I replied.

'I'll do that. Goodbye for now.'

'Thank you, Patrick. Goodbye.'

I put the phone down. Instead of answers, everything had become more complicated. What was Lena doing in East Berlin?

Somehow I felt that Patrick had information that he did not want to share with me for some reason. To suggest that Lena had been abducted as a hoax was in the realms of fantasy. Why he had even suggested that was weird. I was quite certain that Mrs Batty's description of events was accurate. And why a hoax, anyway? My questions came thick and fast but were not matched by answers. As I left my den and crossed the hall, my attention was drawn to Lena's jacket hanging on the coat stand. Underneath, on the rail, her shoes were neatly placed. The sight of them ruled out in my mind the possibility of Patrick's suggestion. Even someone involved in a hoax would have ensured that they wore a pair of shoes.

It was late when I turned in for the night, but at first sleep would not come. I lay awake going through the events of the previous week or so over and over again. I knew that the few days I had spent with Lena had changed my life. Despite the mystery surrounding her, I knew that I had become quite fond of her. I wanted to have her back, but the big question was how to achieve this. I also wanted to know more about her. I still found it difficult to comprehend that a person who had such a sweet, loving nature could be the double agent Patrick claimed she was. It became clear that a great deal more remained untold.

It was during my pondering of events that an idea came to me. Why not go to Berlin and make a few enquiries for myself? It seemed to be a reasonable thing to do. Fly out late one day, stay two nights and have a day free to poke around and see what I could find out. I remembered that Lena had told me she had a sister there. Perhaps she could tell me more.

With that comforting thought, I at last fell asleep.

Chapter 9

Despite a lack of sleep, I was up early the next morning. I intended to put my plan into action. After a quick breakfast, I was on the telephone to British Airways, one of the few airlines permitted to fly to Berlin, which necessitated flying over East German territory.

I was in luck: the airline could get me onto a late flight that evening. I had been to Berlin several times and had the addresses of some hotels convenient to the centre. I remembered that Germany was one hour ahead of our time, so I took a chance and made enquiries about a room for the night. The first hotel I tried was fully booked, but the second had a room available, which I reserved for three nights. Two full days there would, I thought, be sufficient time to carry out my investigation.

It did occur to me that I had very little to go on. I needed somewhere to start. An idea had been lurking at the back of my mind ever since I had thought of going to Berlin. The bag Lena had brought with her when she arrived at my house might contain some kind of lead, an address or some other form of helpful information. Prying into another person's private affairs was not something I undertook lightly, but somehow the desperation of the situation drove me forward and made me dismiss my morals. I went into the bedroom, where I knew Lena had left the bag. It was still in the same place. I picked it up and tipped the contents onto the bed.

There were a number of personal things, but it was a bundle of papers, together with some envelopes held together with an elastic band, that caught my attention. Carefully I started to delve into the collection. Two items of interest immediately revealed themselves: West German passports. I opened the first one. It was in Lena's name. It occurred to me that wherever her captors had taken her, she could not have required a passport. The second passport was more of a surprise. It was in the name of Anna Bergmann, presumably Lena's sister. The discovery puzzled and concerned me. What was Lena doing with her sister's passport? And how was her sister managing without one? The mystery deepened, together with my anxiety. Was Patrick right after all? Was Lena a spy? I had to find the answers to all my questions somehow.

Putting the passports to one side, I turned my attention to the envelopes. Several of these gave me valuable information. Two were addressed to Lena, and another was for Anna Bergmann at an address in West Berlin. More puzzling was that one of the addresses for Lena was in East Berlin, and the other in West Berlin. I could not believe my luck, because I now had three addresses that were going to be extremely useful. Surely, I figured out, Lena's sister would know where she was. Or perhaps I would encounter a neighbour who might know something. I made a note of all the details I felt I might need and then carefully replaced the contents of the bag and put it back into place.

My next mission was to go to the bank and obtain some money. I drew out much more than I normally would, but I knew from previous visits that foreign currency was a valuable asset in East Germany because it enabled the holder to obtain items that would not be normally available to purchase with East German marks. I also knew from past experience that though my credit card would be useful in West Berlin, it would be of little use in East Berlin, which I now felt sure I would end up visiting.

When I returned to the house, Mrs Batty was there, busy with the vacuum cleaner. I had again forgotten it was one of her days to come to me. Of course, she immediately wanted to know if I had any news about Lena. I had to say that I was still waiting for information. She looked puzzled, and I could understand why: my inability to tell her more most likely conveyed reluctance on my part to let her know what was happening. I told her that I was going to Germany for a few days to try to find out a bit more. Again, I don't think she really believed me. I think she thought that perhaps there was more to everything, or she may even have concluded that I had arranged to see Lena there, but she accepted my explanation without any comment and told me that she would pop into the house from time to time to make sure everything was all right.

Once Mrs Batty had left, I pottered about in my den, dealing with several items urgently requiring attention before my few days' absence. It was well past midday before I got around to making myself a quick snack. While I was eating, it occurred to me that I should let Patrick know what I was doing, just in case he tried to contact me again. I rang the number with the code word again, and the same woman answered. I asked for Patrick, but she advised me that he was on leave for several days. In a way it was a kind of relief, because if he was not at work the chances were that he would not try to contact me and I would not miss out on any vital information he might want to share. I asked the woman if she could take a message, and she agreed. I left a few words stating that I was going to Berlin for several days.

My packing was minimal. My leather shoulder bag just contained my overnight gear, and for good measure, considering the inclement weather that was around, I put in an umbrella and a light raincoat. I made sure that the information I would need when I arrived in Berlin was safely tucked into the side pocket of the bag.

Early in the evening I made my way by taxi to Heathrow, allowing plenty of time to have a leisurely meal at the airport. The flight was on time and I was surprised to see that the aircraft was only half full. The seat alongside me was unoccupied. For

71

most of the journey I went over all the events of the past few days. There were now so many questions to which I had no answers. I had embarked on this trip on the spur of the moment, trusting that once in Berlin I might find some. Little did I suspect what lay ahead.

It was dark by the time we landed at Berlin Tegel Airport. I had been there on previous occasions on business for a company I worked for before I became self-employed, so I knew how to reach the city centre, taking a short bus journey and then the U-Bahn. Once there, I made my way to the hotel. It was now late and there was nothing more I could do that evening. I decided to call it a day.

I had a restless night, listening to the sounds that filtered through the open window, sounds of a city asleep, with some activity going on here and there. Several times I heard some of the more restless animals in the zoo, which was not very far away. In the end I did not fall asleep until well into the night, and as a result I woke up later than I had intended.

It was a bright sunny morning, the sun streaming into the room. After a hearty breakfast I departed on my first mission, to locate the woman I believed to be Lena's sister. This meant a ten-minute journey on the U-Bahn. I had located the street with the aid of a map of Berlin that I had possessed for a number of years. I had been pleased to note that there appeared to be a U-Bahn halt within walking distance of the address I had for Anna. Alighting from the train, I found myself in a residential area with pleasant, tree-lined roads. A five-minute walk took me to the address, which was in a small development of apartments. Here a problem loomed up. The block had a secure entrance. To gain access to the apartments required the visitor to call the resident in question and obtain entry. I rang the bell, but there was no answer. Clearly no one was at home. It occurred to me that perhaps morning was not an ideal time. As I stood outside the entrance to the apartments, wondering what should be my next step, a middle-aged woman appeared, clearly intent on entering the building. She appeared to have a key.

She eyed me up carefully before she spoke. 'Darf ich Ihnen helfen?' ['May I help you?']

I summoned up my best German. 'Ich möchte mit Anna Bergmann sprechen.' ['I wish to speak with Anna Bergmann.']

The woman shook her head. 'Die ist nicht hier.' ['She is not here.']

From a brief conversation with the woman in my limited German, I gathered that Anna had been away for some weeks. The woman was her immediate neighbour.

I thanked the woman and went on my way. If Anna had been away for some weeks, there was no point in hanging around. It would be better to move on. It was already close to midday, so I called in at a small bar close to the U-Bahn station and had a coffee. My next venture would be to seek out the address I had for Lena. This would entail a journey to the other side of Berlin.

My search took me to an area with many Turkish shops and cafés, and the people in the street appeared to be mainly Turkish. I quickly located the block where I believed Lena lived. On the ground floor at street level were a number of shops, some open to the pavement. Close to the entrance to the apartments was a fruit and vegetable stall. As I entered the building, a rather stout man, clearly the proprietor of the stall, who was in the process of serving a customer, eyed me up closely.

Lena's apartment was on the third floor, and though there was a lift I climbed the stairs, which were bounded with iron railings. The building appeared to be quite old and had an air of a past age about it. I guessed it had survived the intensive bombardment of Berlin at the end of the second world war. I found Lena's door and rang the bell. Nothing happened. After a short wait I rang again. Again there was no reply.

Suddenly the door of the apartment next to Lena's opened and a woman's head emerged. She looked at me and announced, 'Die ist nicht hier.'

I asked her if she knew where Lena was. The answer was unhelpful. 'Das weiß ich nicht.' ['I don't know.']

I thanked the woman, and she retreated into her apartment.

There was nothing more to be done. I made my way back down the stairs. It seemed as if my mission to find out more about Lena was not having any success. Two attempts to get more information had not achieved anything.

As I came back out into the sunshine, I glanced at the fruit and vegetable stall. The apples looked inviting and I decided to treat myself. The owner spied me looking and immediately came over to serve me. I selected my proposed purchase and as he put the apples into a bag the man grinned at me. 'You from England? I speak English.' He had a strong accent.

I smiled. 'Yes, I am.'

The man pointed to himself. 'I live three years in London.'

'What part of London?'

'Wembley. I have business there.'

I was about to ask another question when he spoke again. 'You know someone here?' He nodded towards the door I had just emerged from. He quickly added, 'I live here with my family.'

I realised that this could be an opportunity to learn more about Lena. 'I'm looking for Lena Bergmann,' I replied.

The man's face lit up. 'I know her. Very pretty girl.' He grinned again. 'She have many men friends.'

It was not something I welcomed hearing, but I felt that the man might have more information. He appeared to want to talk, and he obviously knew Lena.

'Do you know where she is?' I asked hopefully.

My informant beamed at me. 'I know,' he announced in his broken English. 'She is gone to East Berlin.' He came closer to me and lowered his voice. 'She go there often. I think maybe she have a boyfriend there.' He grinned at me again and gave me a wink.

I gave a fake grin in reply. Again this was not something I wanted to hear.

I paid for the apples and we chatted for a few more minutes. However, despite my prompting it did not appear that the man had any further information to divulge that might be of use to me. While it had been pleasant to talk to someone who actually knew Lena, I suspected that most of what he had told me was merely assumption on his part. I was still finding it hard to see the Lena I knew in the role other people claimed. It was true, though, that to keep an open mind I had to remind myself that I really knew very little about her other than what I had learnt from others. I felt that it was essential for me to meet her on her home territory. Her alleged abduction was another factor to consider. Where did that fit into the picture? From what I had been told and had gleaned so far, Lena was certainly not a prisoner of any kind here in Berlin. This had been confirmed by both Patrick and now her neighbour. It was all a mystery.

By now it was well into the afternoon. It was too late in the day to contemplate crossing the border into East Berlin. As early as possible the next day, I planned, I would pass through the notorious Checkpoint Charlie and enter East Berlin and see what I could find out there.

Chapter 10

The next morning I was up early, as I knew that crossing over into East Germany could take a while. Immediately after breakfast I made my way to Checkpoint Charlie. I had visited East Berlin some years previously as an interlude on a business trip to Berlin, and I was interested to see what had changed over the years.

When I arrived at the checkpoint, there was already a small queue of people waiting to obtain their permits. The process was slow, as the officials carefully scrutinised papers, searched baggage and took their time in issuing the required documentation.

Eventually it was my turn. My passport was checked page by page, I was asked a number of questions, including how long I wanted to stay in the DDR – or Deutsche Democratic Republic, as it is correctly called – where I was going, and so on. I paid the fee and at last my paperwork was issued. I had a permit to stay in the country until midnight that night.

With the formalities over, I walked away from the checkpoint and took stock of my surroundings. A few things had changed since my last visit. A new Palace of the Republic had been built on the banks of the river Spree, which flows through Berlin. It was a rather square glass building without much character, and it acted as a direct contrast to the burnt-out remains of the Dom (cathedral) close by, a reminder of what Berlin had gone through at the end of the second world war, and a sad shadow of its previous splendour.

A striking example of contrast with West Berlin was the lack of traffic. Here the roads were remarkably quiet, and even the shops seemed to keep a low profile.

Though I had a map of East Berlin, I had difficulty locating the address I had there for Lena. I appeared to be in the right street, but the name was completely different. I stopped a pedestrian and in my best German attempted to ask him, but my efforts were in vain. He shrugged his shoulders: he did not know.

By a stroke of luck I spotted a police car parked at the side of the road. Two young policemen in the distinctive East German uniform were just getting out of it. I quickly hurried towards them and politely asked my question. Both eyed me suspiciously.

'Ausweis, bitte.' ['Passport, please.']

I handed over my passport and day permit. Both were carefully scrutinised. At last they were handed back to me. One of the policemen spoke good English. He asked me, 'Are you a tourist, or on business?'

A reply was a bit difficult. 'A tourist, but I wish to see somebody here.'

'What connection do you have with the person you wish to see?'

That one was even more difficult. My reply was a bit of a fib. 'She is a girl I hope to marry.' I added, 'I cannot find the address where she lives.'

I was not prepared for the next question. 'What is her name?'

Still puzzled, I answered, 'Lena Bergmann.'

I detected a brief glance between the two policemen. Suddenly one of them asked me, 'What is the address where you wish to go?'

I told him.

He raised his hand and pointed down the street. 'One, two, three, fourth street. That is it.'

I thanked him and received a nod by way of a reply. I continued on my way. The two men watched me for a few seconds, before proceeding on their own business.

It was several minutes' walk to the street I had been directed to, but when I reached it, I was surprised to see that the name on the plate was different from the one I had down as Lena's address. Still puzzled, I started to walk along it. Surely the policeman could not have been wrong.

It was a narrow street filled mainly with apartment blocks and a few small shops. It was clearly one of the older streets of Berlin that had escaped war damage. An elderly man with a wizened face was sweeping the pavement. He had his eyes on me, perhaps recognising that I was a stranger. His gaze was more one of interest than suspicion. I stopped and asked him if he could tell me where Lena's address was.

He put his broom down on his collection trolley and beckoned me to follow him. A dozen paces brought us to a broad alleyway between two buildings. My helper grinned at me and pointed down the alleyway. I was surprised that he spoke quite good English.

'It is here. The name of the street has been changed quite recently.'

That explained a lot. I was about to thank him, but he spoke again. 'You are English. Yes?' He was smiling at me.

He pointed to himself. 'I was prisoner in England in the war. I was Luftwaffe pilot and I was captured.'

'I'm sorry about that,' I replied.

He grinned at me. 'I work on farm – learn English.' He paused. 'You know somebody who lives here?' He nodded towards the alleyway.

'Yes. A young lady I know quite well.'

At that instant a middle-aged woman emerged from the alleyway. My questioner was immediately alert. 'This lady lives here. Maybe she knows your friend.'

Without waiting for any response from me he spoke to the woman. 'Guten Tag, Frau Weber.' He gestured towards me as he asked her whether she might be able to help me locate my friend.

The woman looked at me, perhaps a bit suspiciously. 'Wie heißt sie?' she asked, studying me closely.

'Lena Bergmann,' I replied hopefully. If the woman knew Lena, I might obtain some information about her whereabouts.

On hearing my reply, the woman's attitude changed rapidly. 'Lena Bergmann,' she almost spat in disgust.

There was a moment of uncomfortable silence between the three of us. I tried desperately to think of something to say, but I was hampered by my limited German. It was the woman who spoke next. She drew closer to me and informed me in a low voice that the police had come and taken her away.

I struggled to digest this new information. I started to speak, but the woman did not want to answer any more questions. Before I could get the words out, she declared that that was all she knew. With a wave of her hand as if to brush over the incident, she went on her way.

The street cleaner looked at me oddly. Feeling embarrassed and frustrated, I realised that there was nothing more I could do. I could tell that the woman did not want to get involved. She had no idea who I was, and it would have been inadvisable for her to do anything that might bring her to the attention of the security officials.

There was clearly no more help or information available. I hastily thanked the street cleaner and went on my way. It seemed that each piece of information I received made finding out more about Lena extra difficult and appeared to deepen the mystery surrounding her. If she had been arrested by the East German police, who had abducted her from my doorstep? How did she get back to East Berlin?

I walked slowly away. It seemed as if my visit had been in vain. It was now difficult to see what more I could glean unless I went to the police, something I was loath to do in East Germany. It was perhaps better to wait for Patrick to come up with more information.

I decided to spend the remainder of the time available to me exploring a bit more of the city. In the area I was in at present, I never seemed to be far out of sight of the Berlin Wall, which dominated the area.

I had been walking for perhaps an hour, taking in my surroundings in my own quiet way. At one point I stopped at a small café and had a cup of rather insipid coffee, served in silence by a young girl. A man, clearly the manager or owner of the establishment, watched me from behind the counter. I wondered vaguely if the café was private or state-owned. Private establishments were not common in the communist state, but they did exist. With its bare tables and functional appearance, the place had little of the finesse of the conventional German Konditorei. I spent about ten minutes drinking my coffee. There were several other people in the café, all consuming refreshments in silence, with the occasional glance at me. I guessed they had quickly come to the conclusion that I was not from East Germany.

I finished my drink and left the café. It was now early afternoon and I decided to return to West Berlin. I started to walk back in the direction of the checkpoint, realising how far I had ventured from it on my exploration. I found myself on a rather quiet road lined by insignificant buildings interspersed with several wartime ruins.

At first I did not take any notice of the police car that drove slowly past me. I was alerted when it stopped a couple of dozen yards ahead. By the time I reached it two young policemen had emerged and were almost blocking my route. They greeted me with a polite 'Guten Tag'. Next came the usual demand to see my passport and day pass. Assuming at this stage that this was just a routine check, I was happy to oblige.

I was shocked when one of the policemen, in good English, said, 'Mr Mallon, please come with us.'

I managed to get out a reply. 'What have I done? I am a tourist and a British citizen. My papers are in order.'

The reply I received was not enlightening or helpful. 'I understand, sir, but you must come with us.'

Questions raced through my head. First, what had I done to receive this attention? And second, what was I being accused of? 'But why?' I protested.

'Just some routine questions, sir. We will not keep you long.'

Why was this happening to me? Twice within the space of a few hours I had been quizzed by the police. Now they wanted to take me somewhere. I knew refusal was not an option. Perhaps the best thing would be to go along and find out what it was all about and complain afterwards.

'Very well,' I answered, 'but I am in a hurry.'

'I understand, sir. We will not keep you long.' He opened one of the rear doors of the car and gestured to me to get in. Reluctantly I complied, and the two policemen took their seats in the front.

After perhaps a mile or so the car turned into a side road and then into a passageway between two tall, rather grim-looking buildings. We pulled up in a courtyard where several other police cars were parked. The two men got out and the door was once again held open for me. In silence we entered one of the buildings, and I was ushered along a maze of corridors with closed doors on either side. At last a door was opened and I was ushered into a small room, which was empty except for a wooden table and several chairs.

'Wait in here, please,' came the instruction.

I felt that at this stage that I had little option and obligingly sat down on one of the chairs. My two escorts left and closed the door.

I could not have waited more than five minutes before the door was opened again and a middle-aged man in plain clothes entered, a file of papers in his hand. I leapt to my feet.

The man held out his hand and greeted me in excellent English. 'Good afternoon, Mr Mallon.'

I shook his hand. He gestured towards the seat. 'Please sit down.'

I sat down and waited while he seated himself opposite me and placed his papers on the table, before I asked the question that was uppermost in my mind. 'Can you tell me why I have been brought here? I am not aware that I have broken any law.'

'We just want to ask you some questions.'

My patience was slowly evaporating. 'What about?' I asked. 'I am a British citizen, here as a tourist. I have no other connection with East Germany.'

As soon as the words were out of my mouth, I knew I had made an error.

My remark was received with a frown and a reprimand. 'I think you should remember to use the correct name, the German Democratic Republic.'

'I'm sorry. It was a foolish mistake to make.'

My interrogator nodded and opened the file he had brought with him. He stared at me for a few seconds before he spoke. 'You arrived here this morning, and since then you have been making enquiries about a woman named Lena Bergmann. Is that correct?'

A shock wave crept over me. In the short space of time I had been here, the police had already obtained details about me and what I had been up to. I wondered which of the people I had spoken to had been the informer. Everyone I had engaged with had appeared so friendly and helpful. It was an eye opener into the way the communist state worked and why some people were reluctant to talk to strangers.

My reply to the question was brief. 'Yes. That is correct.'

'What is your connection with this woman?'

I felt I had to answer carefully and be sparing with the truth. 'I met her in London and would like to see her again.'

For a moment the man seemed puzzled by my words, but he recovered quickly and immediately posed another question. 'Are you aware that Miss Bergmann has been proved to have conducted spying activities against the DDR?'

'No. I was not aware of that.'

The man glanced at his papers briefly. 'You must understand that in these circumstances anyone visiting the DDR and making enquiries, as you have done, about this person, is of interest to our security officials.'

I tried to speak calmly. 'Yes, I understand that, but my enquiries were purely from a desire to see Lena again. I learned only this morning that she had been arrested.'

The man's reply was quick. 'That is correct. She was arrested by this department.'

'Is she here? Can I see her?'

My question received a shake of the head and a terse reply. 'I am afraid that is no longer possible.'

'Why? I have nothing to hide. I am just a friend of Lena's.'

I was not prepared for the shock that came next. The man stared at me coldly. When he spoke again, his words stunned me.

'I am sorry. Lena Bergmann is dead.'

Chapter 11

There was silence between us for several seconds. The words I had just heard did not immediately sink in. It all seemed so unreal. I struggled to compose another question, but in the end all I managed to get out was, 'But how?'

My interrogator showed no emotion as he calmly replied. 'She was shot while attempting to escape.'

I tried to absorb the information I had just received.

'I am sorry,' he repeated, clearly without any feeling.

Still in a state of shock, I asked, 'Can I see her?' Somehow that seemed to be the right thing to do.

The officer appeared surprised at my request. 'I will enquire whether it can be arranged. Please wait here.' With that he stood up and left.

I remained in the room for what seemed to be a long time. There was no window, so no natural light entered the gloomy space; the only illumination was from a single light bulb that dangled above the table. The walls of the room had been painted a dull cream colour; the floors were plain boards. The whole place had a claustrophobic feel.

Eventually my interrogator returned, accompanied by a young uniformed policeman. He remained standing in the doorway and addressed me. 'This officer will take you to see the body of Lena Bergman.'

I immediately stood up, assuming that the 'interview' was over. I was slightly incorrect.

The senior officer eyed me up sternly. 'We do not require you any further at present, Mr Mallon, but I must warn you that any attempt you make to enquire further into the activities of Lena Bergman will be viewed with suspicion by the DDR and will require investigation.'

I nodded acceptance of the statement and turned to leave; there did not seem to be any point in making any more comments. No further conversation took place as I followed the young policeman out of the room.

My escort guided me through the maze of corridors to the outside world. Once there we crossed the yard to the street outside. We walked for perhaps two hundred yards and then turned into an entrance between two buildings. This short passage led us into a small yard surrounded by buildings. My escort led me to a door that had no marking to indicate where it led. He thumped on the solid metal. It seemed a long time before anything happened. We waited in silence, each absorbed in his own thoughts. Suddenly the door was opened halfway and a grey-haired man in a white coat looked out at us.

The young policeman addressed him, with a nod to indicate me. I could just about understand what he said. 'This man wishes to see the body of Lena Bergmann. It is in order that you show him. Comrade Yashov has granted permission.'

The man in the white coat stared at me but said nothing. The officer nodded to me and turned to leave, his part in the proceedings clearly complete.

'Danke schön,' I said.

He replied with the customary polite 'Bitte schön', and departed.

I turned my attention to the man in the white coat. In the best German I could command, I explained my mission, making sure to stress that I had the permission of the police. The man continued to stare at me for several seconds without speaking. I was just coming to the conclusion that he had not understood my most likely bad German, when he responded.

First, he shook his head. It was not possible at present to comply with my request. I should come back tomorrow.

I tried to explain that I could not do that, as I was only in the DDR until midnight. I was not expecting his next response.

'Haben Sie Geld?' ['Do you have any money?']

I asserted that I did, wondering where the conversation was leading.

'Dollar?' The question was asked almost eagerly.

I shook my head. 'Pfund Sterling,' I replied.

The attendant thought for a few seconds. Suddenly he spoke again. 'Kommen Sie heute Abend um acht Uhr hierher. Es wird Sie zwanzig Pfund kosten.' ['Come here at eight this evening. It will cost you twenty pounds.']

I realised at once what was happening. Evidently the attendant had seen in me an opportunity. If citizens of the DDR can get hold of foreign currency, they can go to a special shop and buy goods that are not otherwise available to them. It seemed that dollars were preferred over pounds. I felt that in the circumstances there was little I could do other than accept his terms.

I agreed the time and fee and left. It was a bit of a blow, as it was barely four in the afternoon, so I had another four hours to spend doing something.

I decided to look for somewhere to eat. I had not had any food since my early breakfast and I was now feeling decidedly peckish.

I wandered through the streets to where there were some shops and found a kind of café. It was a self-service establishment, rather reminiscent of a canteen or army dining room, bare and devoid of any decoration. I managed to purchase a plate of sausages and potatoes.

I took my time over the meal. Eventually I left the café and decided to do a little more exploring. As I walked, I took in the old buildings that still existed, and occasionally passed ruins of others that had been bombed during the war. Berlin had been badly battered as the Russian army closed in on the city. After a short while I became aware of the feeling that I was being followed. Several times, the same person had appeared behind me, keeping his distance. At one point I entered a large shop in order to have a look around. I was not surprised to see my tracker enter behind me and pretend to be taking an interest in something on display. Here I was able to view him more closely. He was middle-aged, dressed in a shabby raincoat, and he carried a large briefcase. He certainly did not look like a policeman.

I contrived to give him the slip by diving out of the shop when his view of me was blocked by a small crowd. Once outside I walked very quickly away from the area. When I eventually looked round, he was nowhere to be seen. My strategy appeared to have been successful.

It was just coming up to eight o'clock when I returned to the quiet street where the mortuary was. There was nobody around as I knocked on the metal door. It was immediately opened halfway and the attendant I had encountered in the afternoon peered out. On seeing me he opened the door wider and motioned to me to enter. I found myself in a brightly lit passageway. He closed the door and then to my surprise held out his hand. Clearly he wanted his money before showing me anything. I extracted the twenty-pound note I had ready in my pocket and handed it to him. He looked at it, held it up to the light and gave a nod instead of a verbal reply.

Having secreted the payment safely away, he turned round and started to walk down the corridor. Not a word had passed between us, and I assumed I was expected to follow. We did not walk very far. At the end of the corridor was a door, which the attendant opened. He touched a light switch. I followed him into a large room that was lined from floor to ceiling with white tiles. There was a peculiar smell in the room, reminiscent of antiseptic. Several long benches stood there, each occupied by a still form enveloped in a white sheet. The attendant went to a bench at the end of the room and carefully drew back the sheet, holding it up so that I could observe the person lying there, at the same time averting his gaze to another part of the room.

I stared in disbelief. There was no mistaking that this was Lena. She looked strangely peaceful lying there. It seemed unbelievable that this was the same person who only a few days previously had lain in my arms. I wondered what she had gone through since her abduction from my house.

I did not remain there for long. Lena had come into my life out of the blue and I had enjoyed every minute of my brief interlude with her, but that had now abruptly ended. It was a very sad ending and one that I did not understand. There was still so much about her that was remote from me. I realised that now I had to accept that Patrick's description of her had been correct. People do not usually get shot by the police unless they are up to something. I knew now that I had seriously misjudged the situation. But at the same time that realisation clashed with the memory of the sweet girl I had known for just a few short weeks.

Almost overwhelmed by my thoughts and memories, I nodded to the attendant and he quickly replaced the sheet over Lena's face. My request had been fulfilled.

The attendant showed me out in silence. At the door I thanked him and he nodded by way of a reply. As I turned away I heard the door close with a clang.

Sadness weighed heavily on me as I walked away from the area. My mission in East Berlin was now complete. The end result had not been what I expected when I arrived, and now all I wanted was to leave the place as quickly as possible. I made my way towards the checkpoint. I just wanted to get through the barrier and return to my hotel.

Dusk was now approaching. At first I did not take any notice of the large black car driving slowly past me. Then I noticed that it appeared to be cruising along slowly ahead of me. There was hardly any other traffic on the road. I saw the car pull into the kerb and stop. As I approached, a rear window was lowered, and when I was alongside a voice rang out in English.

'Mr Mallon, I would like to speak with you.'

I paused in my walking. Was this again some sort of police interview? The car did not look like a police car. I peered in and saw a smartly dressed man. I responded to the request with a simple 'Yes'.

The man emerged from the car and held out his hand. 'Forgive me, Mr Mallon, for this unexpected involvement in your affairs, but I think a short conversation between us could be beneficial to us both.'

I paused as I studied the individual in front of me. He certainly did not look like a policeman. I judged him to be older than me, perhaps forty-plus to my thirty years. He spoke perfect English in a slightly high-pitched voice. Something urged caution in my response, though at the same time I was intrigued how somebody in the DDR could recognise me.

'I don't think I know you,' I replied rather coldly.

He immediately expressed his concern. 'My dear fellow, I do apologise. Please forgive me. My name is Max Meyer. Do call me Max.'

'Can you tell me what you wish to talk to me about?' I asked, still cautious.

He smiled. 'Indeed I can. I think we have a common interest in a certain lady – Lena Bergmann.'

'Really?' I replied, still suspicious and guarded.

Max smiled at me again. 'Mr Mallon, I understand your concern. Being accosted in the street!' He laughed. 'Coupled with English reserve.'

'Please explain what you want from me,' I demanded, still quite serious.

'I do assure you that I mean well,' he replied. He hesitated and then looked around quickly before continuing. 'Look, we can't talk out here in the street. Why don't we go somewhere more congenial? I know an excellent bar not far from here.'

I was still wary of his intentions. 'Are you from the Stasi [secret police]?' I demanded.

Max threw back his head and laughed. 'I can assure you I am not!'

In spite of this assurance, I hesitated to accept his invitation, yet at the same time I wondered what interest this man had in Lena and what he wanted from me. After a short period of consideration, my curiosity overcame my caution. In the meantime Max had been watching me intently, waiting for an answer.

'I cannot spend a lot of time. I have to return to West Berlin before midnight,' I replied.

'I will keep our chat brief. Please join me. We can drive there. It's only a short distance.' As he spoke, Max ushered me into the back seat of the car and climbed in beside me.

I had already noticed that another man, clearly an employee or a chauffeur, was in the front of the vehicle. This fitted in with the air of prosperity and wealth that Max Meyer had about him.

We drove for no more than four or five minutes through almost deserted streets. Eventually we turned down a side street and pulled up outside a rather drab-looking building. There was no indication of what it might be. Max announced, 'This is it. We are here.'

We both got out of the car. The driver was told to wait and I followed Max into the building. Once I was inside I could see that it was some kind of restaurant, but it was a much more elaborate place than the one I had eaten in earlier in the day. It was clear that Max was well known there. A man I took to be the head waiter greeted him by name and ushered us to a table.

Max turned to me and gave a slight smile. He spoke in a low voice. 'This is an establishment solely for Communist Party members. Fortunately, I am honoured with special membership.'

I understood his explanation. In the DDR, members of the Communist Party did have special privileges. I wondered vaguely how Max Meyer qualified for membership.

We sat down at a table. My host offered to buy me a meal, but I wanted to keep the meeting short, so I insisted on just having a cup of coffee.

I endeavoured to keep the small talk to a minimum. 'You said you wanted to talk about Lena Bergman,' I began.

'Indeed, yes. I am most anxious to contact the lady.' I was surprised by his answer. Clearly he did not have the information I was in possession of.

'You sound as if you know her quite well,' I ventured.

Max gave me another one of his smiles. 'Yes, you could say that. Our relationship goes back a number of years.'

I was about to ask another question, but Max chipped in first. 'How long have you known her?'

'Not very long. She stayed with me for a short time recently.' I thought I detected a brief indication of puzzlement in Max, but I could not be certain. 'What do you want her for?' I demanded, determined to keep the conversation focused.

'She is in danger. I believe I can help her.'

I began to speak again, but before I could say anything Max directed another question at me. 'You were interviewed by the police today. What was the reason for that? Was it in connection with Lena?'

'They wanted to know what my interest was in her,' I replied.

'Did they tell you where she was?'

I hesitated. Clearly Max had no idea that Lena was dead. I was unsure whether I should tell him. In the end I decided that I should. After all, I reasoned, in a short while I would be safely back in West Berlin. On top of that, I guessed the information would eventually be released by the authorities for propaganda purposes.

I cleared my throat. Max was looking at me, eager for my answer.

'I was informed that she was dead,' I replied calmly.

Max stared at me in disbelief. 'Are you sure? What else did the police tell you? This is most disturbing news.'

'I was told she had been shot while trying to escape.' I paused. 'I have seen her body.'

The news seemed to have shocked Max badly. Almost to himself he spoke a few words. 'This news puts a totally different aspect on things. I thought I could get to her before this happened.'

I decided to pursue my own agenda. 'What did she do?' I asked.

Max drew closer to me across the table. He spoke softly. 'Lena was a very dangerous woman. She lived a dangerous life.'

I wrestled to reconcile this statement with the memory of the Lena I had spent a short time with. 'But she seemed such a quiet, sweet girl,' I remarked.

He looked at me and smiled. 'There were two sides to her. That was why she was so good at what she did.'

'You mean spying?'

Max nodded. 'Something like that.'

'Was that why she was abducted from my house a few days ago?' I asked.

Max shook his head. 'That was a different person.'

It was my turn to be shocked. 'What do you mean?' I demanded. 'Are you trying to tell me that it wasn't Lena?'

Max smiled again. 'I'm afraid so. Lena Bergmann has been in Germany all this year. I can vouch for that.'

Chapter 12

Max's words astounded me. They made the whole situation even more unbelievable.

I stammered a reply. 'Are you... are you trying to tell me that the person I had in my house wasn't Lena Bergman?'

Max nodded. 'I'm sorry to have to tell you that the person you thought was Lena was actually her sister Anna.'

I struggled to comprehend what I had just heard. Why should two sisters swap roles? There was also Boris Smirnov to consider. How did he fit into the equation? He seemed to have been unaware of the change. Or had he also been part of the conspiracy – if that was what it was? The questions raced through my brain. The bottom line appeared to be quite clear: I had been duped both by Boris and by Lena's sister for reasons unknown. I had just been a pawn in their game. There was also Patrick's side of events to consider. He appeared to have been quite convinced that I had been entertaining Lena Bergmann. Or was he another part of the plot, whatever that was?

Max had been looking at me intently as I went over all these things in my mind. He continued drinking his coffee as he scrutinised me. Eventually he broke the silence between us. 'I'm extremely sorry if my information has upset you in any way.'

'It's all right,' I replied. 'Thank you for telling me.'

'The two sisters are remarkably similar in looks,' he continued. 'A stranger would be unable to tell them apart.'

I nodded acceptance of the statement, but I wanted to hear more from Max. 'You appear to have known Lena Bergmann quite well. Do you also know her sister?' I asked.

'In the past I knew both of them quite well.'

'Is Anna also engaged in spying activities?'

Max shrugged. 'Perhaps.'

'Do you know where she is now?'

Max's answer was immediate. 'No.'

The speed of his reply told me something. It seemed to me that Max Meyer knew a great deal more than he was going to confide in me. Suddenly I felt overcome by the futility of the whole thing. I had come to Berlin seeking a girl I had only known for a few weeks. I had become enamoured with her good looks and charm and had been chasing a dream. I had been completely taken in by both Boris Smirnov and somebody calling herself Lena who was apparently not Lena, but her sister Anna. In a way I had made a bit of a fool of myself. Now I just wanted to leave Berlin and forget the whole thing.

I finished my coffee. Putting the cup down, I decided it was time for me to go. Nothing more could be gained from staying any longer. In any case, the clock was ticking on towards midnight.

I stood up and held out my hand. 'If I cannot assist you any further, I had better take my leave.'

Max immediately jumped up. He grasped my hand. 'My dear fellow, allow me to take you. My car is waiting outside.'

I shook my head. 'No, thank you. I prefer to walk.' I was growing a bit tired of his patronising approach to me.

He did not try to persuade me, for which I was thankful. I quickly made my exit, leaving him to watch me walk out of the restaurant. He appeared to be deep in thought.

Outside it was dark. Max's car was still parked outside. The driver glanced at me as if wondering whether I required his services, but he did not speak to me.

I hurried away from the area. I was quite confident that I could find my way back to the checkpoint, and I made haste in that direction.

I had been walking for about ten minutes when I again became aware that I was being followed. With careful scrutiny to ensure that I was not making the other person aware of my observation, I established that it was the same man I had seen earlier in the day and had shaken off in the shop.

I started to walk faster, but my shadow also increased his pace, always keeping the same distance from me. In an effort to shake him off, I dived into a side street. It was to no avail. The man followed me.

Suddenly a black car appeared from behind us. It was the only one on the quiet street. It stopped alongside the man and I saw him get in. The car sped off into the night. I was surprised a few minutes later when it passed me going in the opposite direction. I could see at least three people in it. It passed me and then disappeared out of sight down another side street.

I turned round and retraced my steps to my original route and the one I felt I knew. I was becoming a bit concerned that time was running out for me to return to the checkpoint much before the deadline. I guessed it was a good twenty-minute walk away. A few minutes later I felt the first drops of rain. This was a concern, because I had left my raincoat and umbrella in the hotel. I turned up the collar of my jacket and pressed on, hoping that the weather would not develop into a heavy fall of rain.

I had been walking in this way for about five minutes when I heard a woman's voice somewhere close by.

She addressed me in a hushed tone in English, but with a German accent. 'Tim Mallon, please come here, quickly!'

I stopped and looked in the direction of the voice. It came from a dark alleyway. I could just make out the figure of a woman of about my own age. She was beckoning me frantically. She spoke again. 'Please come. You are in danger.'

I stared in disbelief. So many people seemed to know my name and appeared intent on meddling in my affairs. Something about the woman made me hesitate. Who was she, and what did she mean?

'What do you mean, I am in danger?' I asked.

'I cannot explain in detail now, but if you continue you will be arrested. Please come with me. I can help you escape.' The invitation was accompanied with more frantic beckoning.

I shook my head. 'What do you mean, I will be arrested? I've done nothing wrong. I'm a tourist. Who are you? How do you know my name?

The woman emerged from the alleyway. She grabbed my arm. 'Please believe me. I want to help you. I know you are in danger here. Please let me help you.'

I gazed at her. It all seemed so bizarre. I wondered vaguely if she was a prostitute anxious to get her hands on some western currency. She did not look or for that matter act like a prostitute.

Perhaps she read my thoughts. 'I know you must wonder why I do this, but you are in danger here and I can help you get away. Please believe me. My man is close by with a car. We can take you to safety.'

I glanced at my watch. 'I'm in a hurry,' I explained. 'I have to get to the checkpoint before midnight.'

The woman shook her head violently. 'No, no! It is not safe. Please do not go to the checkpoint.'

She tried to pull me towards the alleyway, but I managed to resist her.

'Who are you? How do you know so much about me?' I asked.

'My name is Meika. My man and I can help you to safety. We can help you and we need your help.' She paused and drew close to me, saying in a near-whisper, 'We know you came here looking for Anna. We know where she is, and you can help us rescue her.'

I found myself struggling to quite comprehend what was happening. I had spent a whole day searching in vain for the woman I loved, and now a complete stranger seemed to have the information I had been seeking. The situation was beginning to stretch my imagination. It was starting to look like the plot of one of my novels, except that this was not fiction – it was real life.

'How do you know all this?' I asked.

Meika gave a half-smile. 'We just know. We knew you were coming to the DDR. We make it our business to find things out. I also know Anna quite well.'

That was interesting. Here was somebody who actually knew her.

Meika still had her hand on my arm. She gave a little tug. 'Please come with us. We can help you. You will be safe.'

'But I am a British citizen. I have committed no crime and I have a valid visa,' I protested.

Meika shook her head. 'That makes no difference in the DDR. You have been asking questions about Lena. That is sufficient for the police to arrest you. Believe me – I know what I am talking about.'

'But the police have already interviewed me,' I replied.

'Since then you have talked to Max Meyer,' Meika replied.

I was stunned by how much information Meika appeared to possess about me. I was pondering a reply when suddenly she gave my arm a jerk. The action was accompanied with just two words. 'Quickly. Police.'

It was a bit of a turning point. I found myself following Meika into the alleyway. A quick glance over my shoulder indicated the source of her concern. Further down the street a police car had appeared, its lights flashing.

I hurried after Meika, carried away with a kind of panic. The alleyway was short and we soon arrived at a building, or rather the remains of it, as there were only a few walls standing. It was another relic from the war.

Meika picked her way amongst the ruins, following what appeared to be a well-used path, clearly a shortcut used by local people. The rain that had threatened earlier was now starting to fall quite heavily, making the way muddy and slippery.

Eventually we emerged into a quiet road. A small car was waiting there with its engine running, lights on and the passenger door open. Meika urged me on as she hurried over to it. 'Quickly, we must go away from here before the police look for us.'

'But I have only a short time before I have to leave,' I protested.

'You cannot go to the checkpoint. The police will be waiting for you. They are also searching for you. You must come with us. We will look after you. We also have to rescue Anna.'

As she spoke, Meika pushed me into the back seat of the car. A man of about her age was sitting in the driving seat.

'This is Kurt, my man,' Meika announced.

The driver turned round, smiled and greeted me as Meika climbed into the seat beside him. Meika slammed the car door and we sped off.

We drove through almost deserted streets. There was no conversation between Meika and Kurt. I also sat in silence. Everything had happened so fast. One minute I had been walking to the checkpoint, contemplating my visit to the DDR and looking forward to a hot bath and perhaps a meal at the hotel. The next instant I had been virtually kidnapped by two young people who appeared to know a lot about me and what lay ahead for me if I did not comply with their demands. It all felt like some spy novel, except that everything was real and I was a major player in some sort of escapade of which I had little knowledge.

After about ten minutes the car turned into a side street with tall buildings on either side. We drove to the end, where some apartment blocks stood. These had clearly been built since the war, because they were of the usual drab, functional design employed by various communist states in recent years to house their populations.

Kurt stopped the car in front of one of the buildings and Meika jumped out. She turned to me with a smile. 'This is where we live. You will be safe here.'

I reluctantly followed my two alleged rescuers into the building. I glanced at my watch as we entered the lit hallway. It was already past midnight. I was now illegally in the DDR. My spontaneous action in following Meika and Kurt meant that I now had little option other than to tag along with them. There was also Anna to think about.

Meika noticed me looking at my watch. She gave me a little smile. 'Don't worry. We will get you out of the DDR safely.'

I made no comment. We climbed several flights of stairs and then walked along a corridor, eventually stopping in front of a door. Kurt opened it and we entered the apartment.

Meika turned to me. 'Welcome to our home.'

The apartment was quite small and appeared to consist of a small lounge, a bedroom, a tiny kitchen and a bathroom.

'Please sit down,' Meika said, gesturing towards a sofa.

I sat down and looked around me while she and Kurt trotted back and forth taking off their coats and Meika busied herself getting food out and setting a nearby table. Snippets of conversation came my way. Meika asked me if I was hungry, to which I replied, 'A little.' It was true: I had eaten little all day.

At one point, when Kurt left the room for a few seconds, Meika turned to me and whispered, 'I'm sorry. Kurt doesn't speak very much English.' I had already noticed this. He appeared to be friendly, but rather shy.

Just before we were ready to sit down to eat, Kurt asked me, 'Nimmst du Bier oder Wein?' [Will you have beer or wine?] I thought it was interesting that he used the familiar form 'du', rather than the more formal 'Sie'. From my knowledge of

German I was aware that the familiar form is normally used only for family, close friends or children.

'Wein, bitte,' I replied.

Meika called me to the table to eat. At the sight of the food, I realised how hungry I was. Bread and cheese were laid out. I tucked in heartily, aided by two glasses of wine.

My situation was eased by the congenial atmosphere and the effect of the alcohol. However, during a lull in the conversation I asked the question that was uppermost in my mind. 'What is the plan now?'

Meika turned and spoke directly to me. 'We have to rescue Anna. We have to do it quickly. She is in danger.'

'How will you do that?' I asked.

She smiled. 'I will explain. We need you to help us. You are an important part of the plan.'

Chapter 13

Meika's words surprised me. How could I be an important part of rescuing Anna? Her statement also assumed that I was willing to be part of the attempt.

'How can that be?' I asked.

Meika was quick to explain. 'We are known to Anna's captors. They would recognise us immediately. We have to work with somebody who is a stranger.'

'Do you know where Anna is?'

Meika nodded. 'Yes, we do.'

I was going to ask another question, but Meika continued. 'The police interviewed you today. What did they tell you about Lena?'

This was a difficult one. I took my time to think up a suitable answer. I wondered how much Meika and Kurt knew about Lena. Did they know she was dead? All the time they were both watching me intently.

I responded with a question of my own. 'What do you know about her already?'

I felt that my strategy was working. Immediately Meika looked anxious, expectant. She replied quickly, 'Only that she disappeared while on a visit here.'

I knew that I had no other option than to break the news about Lena. 'The police told me she had been shot dead while trying to escape.'

Meika gasped and clutched her hand to her mouth, letting out an agonised 'No'. Kurt, who, though he had some difficulty speaking English appeared to understand it, showed immediate shock and concern.

Meika asked me, 'How can we be certain that this is true?'

'I have seen her body,' I explained.

Meika shook her head. 'Anna will be very upset. They were very close.'

'How well did you know Lena?' I asked.

Meika spoke slowly. 'I didn't know Lena all that well. I know Anna much better.'

I wanted to know more about the two sisters. 'What was Lena like?' I queried.

'Though they were identical twins and it was almost impossible to tell them apart, they were quite different in character. Anna is quiet and thoughtful. Lena was more outgoing.'

I was determined to find out more. 'Do you know why Anna came to England?'

Meika shook her head. 'No. It was a bit of a mystery. She just said she was going to London for a few days.'

'Do you know Boris Smirnov?'

Meika looked puzzled. 'Not really. I met him once when I visited Anna.'

I wondered whether she was aware of who Anna had been with in England. I felt I must enlighten her. 'Anna was living with Boris before she came to stay with me.'

Meika was clearly surprised to hear this. 'I didn't know that,' she remarked.

The mystery surrounding Anna and her relationship with Boris remained unsolved. Meika appeared not to mind me asking questions, so I continued. 'Do you know who took Anna by force from my house?'

Meika nodded straight away. 'Of course. It was all arranged by Max Meyer.'

It was my turn to be surprised. 'But he told me he didn't know,' I stressed.

Meika smiled. 'He would do that. He wants to use Anna to enhance his own position with the high-ups in the DDR administration. He is a very dangerous man. He knew the Stasi wanted to talk to Lena. He thought Anna would lead him to her.'

I was puzzled by this explanation. 'But why?' I asked. 'What's in it for Max Meyer?'

Meika thought for a couple of seconds before answering. When she did it was with a shrug of her shoulders. 'Perhaps money,' she replied.

It all seemed unreal. I had come to East Germany to try to find the whereabouts of a girl called Lena. Now I seemed to have got myself involved in something much bigger. On top of that I was now in the country illegally, having exceeded the time limit on my pass. I glanced at my watch again. It was well after midnight.

'I should have been back in West Berlin by now,' I observed gloomily.

Meika shook her head. 'It would have been dangerous for you to try to return. The police would have detained you again. Max Meyer will have told them something about you that was of interest to them. These people trust nobody.'

This was not comforting news. 'So, what happens now?' I asked.

Meika smiled. 'Don't worry. We will help you escape.'

Considering that she and Kurt had been responsible for my delay, it seemed the least that they could do. I wondered how they were going to accomplish this.

'We also have to free Anna as soon as possible,' Meika commented.

Talking about Anna once again brought back the fondness I still felt for her despite the reality that I had been misled by both her and Boris. At the same time, deep down within me was a desire to get to the truth.

This prompted my next question. 'How do you propose to rescue her?'

'It won't be too difficult. She is being held in an apartment. Your job will be to keep one of her captors talking long enough to allow us to take over.'

It sounded simple enough, but I could not help wondering how it was going to work out in practice.

Meika interrupted my thoughts and any further questions I might have. She regarded me a bit anxiously. 'Will you be all right sleeping on our sofa?' she asked.

I smiled. 'Of course,' I said. I had slept in worse places. It looked as if I would have to accept the arrangements, as I was now a fugitive from the authorities and there seemed to be no other option.

Half an hour later I lay stretched out on the sofa. Stretched out was perhaps not the correct term to use, because my feet dangled over one of the arms.

As I lay there waiting for sleep to come, I went over the day's events. I had entered East Germany in the hope of establishing where Lena was. In the process, I had been interviewed by the police, who told me that Lena was dead, interrogated by Max Meyer, who informed me that the woman I thought was Lena was in fact her twin sister, Anna, and then politely waylaid by Meika and Kurt, who claimed to know where Anna was and wanted me to help them rescue her. What was to happen after that had not been explained to me. On top of everything else, I was now seemingly stranded in East Germany, having exceeded my permitted time there. I guessed I would have some difficult explanations to make.

It had certainly been quite a day.

After a rather uncomfortable night I awoke to the smell of coffee and the sound of someone moving about in the kitchen. I looked at my watch. It was just after six. A few minutes later Kurt appeared from the bathroom. Smiling broadly and with the greeting 'Guten Morgen' he handed me a razor, which was extremely welcome. Almost immediately Meika appeared and with a cheerful 'Good morning' handed me a new toothbrush. It was clearly time to get up.

Twenty minutes later we were all sitting around the breakfast table. Kurt was fully dressed, but Meika was still in her dressing gown. Studying her, I could see that she was quite pretty. I wondered what her story was. Other than that she knew Anna quite well and had spent some time in England, I knew nothing about her. Kurt was a complete mystery. He appeared to be devoted to her.

Over breakfast Meika outlined a little more of the plan to rescue Anna. 'Anna is being held in an apartment a ten-minute drive from here. It is occupied by a couple. The man goes out to work each morning at eight, leaving the woman alone during the day to guard her.'

Meika paused for a second as if to check that I had absorbed this information. I nodded acceptance.

She continued. 'The plan is that as soon as the man has left the building to go to work you will go to the apartment and make enquiries about Anna.'

'What happens after that?' I asked.

Meika appeared quite confident as she outlined the next stage of the operation. 'You will have to keep her talking for long enough to give us time to rush into the apartment and grab Anna.'

All this time Kurt had been listening intently to our conversation. It appeared that Meika was the leader of the two. Kurt rarely spoke, but I could tell that he took a deep interest in everything. I had attempted to engage him in conversation a few times, but his response had always been polite and he was clearly rather shy. I wondered what he thought about the situation.

I probed for flaws in Meika's plan. 'What if Anna is not there?' I asked.

Meika shook her head. 'We know that she is there. But we have to move very quickly. Now that Max Meyer has spoken to you and knows that Lena is dead, he will no longer have any use for Anna.'

'You mean Anna might be in even more danger?'

'Of course. He is a dangerous man and will stop at nothing to achieve what he wants.'

'What work does he do?'

'He buys and sells things – even people.'

'What?'

'He claims to be a businessman, but he will become involved in anything to make money. That is why he wanted Lena.'

'I don't understand. Can you explain?'

'He knew both the DDR and the Americans were anxious to talk to her. After he had seized her he would have negotiated with both parties and passed her over to the one who paid the most.'

This struck me as an odd and highly distasteful situation. 'How does he manage to keep friendly with both the Americans and the DDR administration?' I asked.

Meika smiled. 'He is useful to both sides. He knows a lot of people.'

Our conversation ended abruptly when Kurt looked at the clock and reminded Meika of the time. Quickly gathering our breakfast dishes, she dumped them in the sink, refusing my offer to help. 'We have no time. We must leave now.'

Kurt left the apartment, saying something about getting petrol, and Meika disappeared into the bedroom.

It was a good fifteen minutes before Kurt returned and Meika indicated to me that it was time to go. It did not take us long to reach the ground floor. Kurt had parked the car, a Trabant, close to the entrance to the apartment block, and we all climbed in. The Trabant is produced in East Germany and is a pretty basic affair. It can be seen everywhere, because it is the main car available. Riding in one is quite an experience. It is not very highly regarded and it comes in for a lot of criticism. It appears to be a reliable and sound workhorse, but it lacks many of the sophisticated refinements boasted by western-built cars.

Kurt started the engine and we set off. I was surprised when after a few minutes we suddenly pulled in to the kerb. A young man immediately emerged from a building and joined me on the back seat of the car. Meika introduced him as Hans. 'He is going to help us,' she explained. I received a friendly grin and a handshake from Hans, coupled with 'Guten Tag'.

We drove for about five more minutes and then turned into an area of tall, characterless apartment blocks. Kurt parked the Trabant in a quiet street. Meika turned to me and indicated without words that she and I had to get out of the car. I obeyed her command in silence. The two men remained sitting in the car. I could see Meika carefully looking around to see who or what was there. It was all very quiet. She turned to me and whispered, 'We cannot all enter the building together. It would be too conspicuous. We have to be careful and check the situation.'

I nodded in agreement. I was now completely involved in this cloak-and-dagger operation and on top of fearing for Anna's safety I began to wonder what the outcome would be for me personally. However, there was little time to think of anything except the job in hand. As if to emphasise the necessity for stealth, Meika pulled a scarf from her pocket and wrapped it around her head, partly concealing her face.

We walked a short distance. As we reached the end of one of the blocks, we came to a junction in the road. Meika suddenly grabbed my arm and forced me to stop. Ahead of us was another apartment block and walking along the pavement was a man carrying a briefcase. Meika whispered to me, 'That is the husband going to work. Good. Now we can go in.'

We waited until the man had disappeared and then we walked casually towards the apartment block. Meika made for the entrance door, and we entered a hallway with stairs leading upwards and a lift beside them. Nobody was in sight. Meika whispered to me again. 'This is where Anna is being held. You must go on alone now, but remember that we will be close behind you, waiting for you to get the apartment door open. You must keep the woman talking until we reach you. After that we will take over.'

I was beginning to feel nervous. 'Where do I have to go?' I asked.

'It is on the fifth floor. Apartment number 520. Take the lift.'

'Got it,' I replied.

Meika hesitated for a second, and then she was gone. I was on my own.

I walked over to the lift. It was not in very good condition and at first I had difficulty in finding the correct button. Eventually I located it and the lift began its rumbling ascent. When I emerged on the fifth floor I got into a bit of a panic trying to find the way to the apartment, as the directions on the wall were not very clear. In the end I found the correct corridor and hurried along it, conscious that I had wasted a couple of minutes.

Arriving at apartment 520, I took a deep breath. Now for it, I thought. There did not appear to be a bell of any kind, so I knocked loudly on the door. There was no immediate response. Just as I was about to knock again I heard a sound inside the apartment. The next instant the door opened and a middle-aged woman stood there facing me. She stared at me, clearly waiting for me to speak.

In my best German I announced my business. 'I would like to see Anna Bergmann.'

The woman looked at me suspiciously, shook her head and mumbled something that sounded like 'Nicht hier'.

I was on difficult territory. I knew that I had to keep the conversation, such as it was, going until Meika and her companions arrived.

'But I was told that she was here,' I insisted.

Again the woman shook her head. 'Nein.'

I was about to speak again, when she began to shut the door. I began to panic. I knew I had to keep that door open at any cost. I had no alternative but to put my foot in the way to prevent it from closing. At that moment it was difficult to ascertain which of us was more afraid, the woman with a look of fear on her face, or me with the sinking feeling that my part of the mission was failing.

I need not have worried. The next instant three hooded figures appeared as if from nowhere, brushed passed me, nearly knocking me over, seized the woman and pushed her into the apartment. I followed quickly.

I found myself in an untidy, non-too-clean hallway. My three companions, their faces obscured by improvised masks, were dragging the woman, who was complaining loudly and struggling, into one of the rooms.

'Find Anna.' The voice was Meika's and was directed at me.

I sprang into action. The first door I tried led to an unoccupied bedroom. The next door gave me success. I threw it open wide.

The scene that presented itself shocked me. I was looking into a small bedroom, empty except for a single bed, on which Anna, wearing only panties and a shirt, was lying, visibly alarmed by the sound of us bursting into the apartment. The initial look of concern and fear on her face quickly changed to one of surprise and questioning as I appeared.

'Tim! What are you doing here?'

'We've come to rescue you,' I replied. I was already examining the chain around her ankle. It was secured by a padlock to the metal leg of the bed.

'Where is the key?' I asked.

'That horrid woman has it,' Anna replied, a miserable tone in her voice.

It was enough. I had to get that key. Without it, releasing Anna would be very difficult. Without a word I dashed into the room where the woman was now tied to a chair, a scarf across her mouth suppressing her sounds of protest. I was met by Meika, who was holding a key.

'Quickly!' she exclaimed.

I grabbed the key and went back into the bedroom. A few seconds later I was fitting the key into the padlock, scrutinised closely by Anna and watched anxiously by Meika from the doorway.

I turned the key and removed the padlock. In a few seconds Anna was free. Immediately she jumped off the bed and rummaged beneath it, retrieving a pair of jeans.

'Quickly! We have to go,' urged Meika, turning to leave. I followed her out of the room as Anna hurriedly put her jeans on.

Back in the main room of the apartment, I noticed that Kurt and Hans had already left. The woman directed muffled curses at us with a glare as we hurried past. Anna quickly joined us, viewing her former captor with some disgust. We made haste to the lift and descended to the entrance hall. Meika carefully peered through the outer door to ensure that our escape route was clear before quickly beckoning us forward.

Outside the apartment block she immediately set off at a fast pace, leaving Anna and me to follow. It was now raining and Anna was barefoot, but she strode briskly forward, undaunted by the wet pavement. It only took a few minutes for us to reach the car. Kurt already had the engine running. It appeared that Hans, his part in the mission completed, had made his own way home.

Anna and I squeezed into the cramped back seat of the Trabant and Meika took her place beside Kurt. We had barely settled before Kurt had the car in gear and we were moving off, the engine screaming.

No verbal communication had taken place between us since we left the apartment where Anna had been held. It was I who broke the silence. 'Where are we going?' I asked.

Meika turned to face me. 'We have to get you and Anna away from here to somewhere safe.'

'But I have to go back to West Berlin,' I protested.

Meika smiled. 'Not by the normal exit,' she replied. 'It will no longer be safe.'

I must have looked concerned, because she immediately added, 'Don't worry. We will get you and Anna out of the country.'

I made no reply. My situation was now quite clear. I had been in East Germany less than twenty-four hours and during that time I had become a fugitive from the law. Despite Meika's air of confidence, I was beginning to feel extremely worried about my situation and my safety.

Chapter 14

The Trabant carrying the four of us made its way through the streets of East Berlin. There was no conversation between us. Kurt seemed absorbed and concentrating on his driving, while Meika seemed alert and anxious, continuously looking at the road ahead and what was happening outside. Anna sat beside me, silent and pensive. At one stage I notice her shiver and offered her my jacket. She quickly accepted it and pulled it around her with a quiet 'Thank you'.

I was beginning to feel rather worried about the way things were going. I had been persuaded by Meika to take part in rescuing Anna. That had been achieved, but now I was being dragged off to an unknown destination, without any consultation with me. I decided it was time to ask a few more questions.

'Where are you taking us?' I demanded.

Perhaps the tone of my voice alerted Meika to my concern. She immediately tried to reassure me. 'By now Max Meyer will have alerted the police to your activities. We don't know what lies he will have told them. They will be watching for you at all the border crossings. They will also be looking for Anna. We have to get you both out of the country by a different route. Now we are going to my mother's, where you should both be able to stay until we can make the arrangements.'

It all sounded a bit extreme.

'But do I have to really go to such great lengths to get out of a country where I am a legal tourist – or was until last night?' I asked.

Meika shook her head. 'You don't understand these people and how they work. The smallest thing that they consider to be against the state is of concern to them.'

She sounded sincere, but I was still not completely happy about the situation. There were too many unanswered questions.

'How do you propose to get us out of the country?' I asked.

Meika was quick with her answer. 'We have a route to get you to Denmark. From there you can get back to England. Do you have money?'

'A little.'

'How much?'

'About £150, if I remember correctly.'

Meika nodded. 'It will probably be enough.'

Given the situation, I was glad that the money and my passport nestled safely in my inner pocket. I wondered what would happen to the things I had left in my hotel room, which I should have been vacating that morning. There was also Anna to think about. What was going to happen to her? Thanks to Max Meyer she had arrived in the country illegally. So far we had exchanged no words since the rescue.

I turned to her. 'What about you, Anna? What are you going to do?'

She looked very sad. 'I need to find my sister,' she replied softly.

I now had before me a task I dreaded. I took a few seconds to work out what to say. I held her hand and spoke as kindly as I could.

'Anna, I'm very sorry to have to tell you this, but your sister is dead. I saw her body yesterday. I was told she had been shot trying to escape.'

The next few seconds seemed like minutes. I seemed as if Anna was slowly absorbing the information I had just given her. Then the tears flowed. She covered her face with her hands and sobbed uncontrollably. Her words came in between sobs. 'I knew it would happen one day. I told her what she was doing was dangerous, but she would not listen. She kept saying she was protected.'

I reached out and put my arm around her. She immediately leaned towards me and burrowed her face into my shoulder. I could tell she was crying softly. I held her tightly to try to comfort her. Meika reached over and held her hand for a while. Gradually Anna's sobs ceased, but she remained close to me as I continued to hold her.

Suddenly Kurt attracted our attention. Muttering something, he quickly turned off the main road into a side street.

Meika explained the problem. 'Kurt saw a roadblock ahead of us. The police will be checking cars. We have to divert. They could be looking for you.'

This incident finally convinced me of the danger Anna and I were in. Anna had now become alert to the situation and was looking anxious. I could tell that Meika was concerned. She expressed this to Kurt. It appeared that Kurt was the only one of us who was keeping calm, focusing on his driving.

At one point Meika gave us a few words of explanation. 'Kurt knows another way out of this area, but it will take us longer.'

The diversion certainly appeared to take a long time. We turned this way and that, finding an alternative route. At one stage Kurt turned the car round and went back the way he had come.

'Wrong way,' Meika explained with a trace of a grin. It was a relief to me, as for a split second I thought Kurt had spotted another roadblock.

Eventually we seemed to be back on the correct road. Nobody said anything, but I could feel a general air of relief.

At last we joined a motorway – or Autobahn, to use the correct term. The Trabant increased its pace, its engine note becoming louder. I had only travelled in one briefly on a previous occasion, but I was now moderately impressed with how it dealt with the road conditions.

We were now travelling on one of the original concrete motorways laid down in the years before the second world war, and were leaving behind the obvious trappings of civilisation, the drab and uninteresting blocks of flats. We drove well out into the countryside, including through a forested area where road signs advised travellers to beware of wildlife straying onto the road

After almost two hours Kurt took a turning off the Autobahn. Now we were on a country road with farmland on either side. We passed through a small village consisting of little more than a few houses and a church. Shortly after this the road became quite uneven and bumpy. It appeared to be constructed from stone blocks, which had sunk here and there causing deep potholes. Kurt had to navigate a path to avoid them. Eventually he turned the Trabant down the track leading to what appeared to be a farm standing in some trees well back from the road. We pulled up outside the house. A middle-aged woman wearing an apron watched us arrive.

'My mother,' Meika explained, turning to Anna and me.

We all climbed out of the car. Meika immediately embraced her mother, who was however viewing the rest of us with some suspicion. Meika introduced us, but it was clear that her mother was not at all pleased at the arrival of four uninvited guests. Meika drew her on one side and spoke to her while the rest of us waited by the car.

After three or four minutes they moved back towards us. Meika's mother was expressing herself loudly. 'Why do you bring them here? The police will come and arrest us all.' She waved her arm as if to dismiss us.

It was clear that Meika had been unable to persuade her mother to help us. When she turned back to us, she looked glum. Addressing Anna and me, she explained the situation. 'I am sorry. You cannot stay here. My mother is not happy.'

It was clearly a blow to the arrangements. I wondered what was going to happen next. However, Meika appeared to have everything under control. She motioned us to get back into the car.

We drove away, leaving Meika's mother watching us. We returned to the road and travelled another few miles through farm country. Eventually we came to a house standing on its own. Kurt stopped the car and immediately Meika got out, at the same time asking us to stay in the car. She marched up to the door of the house. It was immediately opened by a young woman about the same age as Meika. It was clear that they both knew each other quite well, because there was much laughter and excitement at the meeting. Meika then disappeared inside the house.

We sat and waited for ten minutes or more. Eventually Meika and the young woman reappeared, accompanied by a middle-aged woman. They were all smiling broadly. This looked much more hopeful than the encounter with Meika's mother. I was beginning to wonder why we had not come here first.

Meika introduced the two women as Maria and her daughter Gerda. Maria smiled broadly, but it was Gerda who did all the talking. 'Of course you can stay with us,' she said to Anna and me. 'You are very welcome.'

I thanked her and remarked upon her command of English.

'I learned it at school,' she explained, adding sadly, 'but these days I don't have any opportunity to speak English.'

Her mother ushered us into the house. Within a few minutes we all found ourselves seated around a large table in the kitchen, while Maria and Gerda hurriedly produced a meal. Bottles of beer were brought in for Kurt and me. They were large, and by the time I had finished mine I was beginning to feel more relaxed about the whole proceedings.

As we ate, I managed to piece together a better picture of the whole situation I was involved in. It appeared that Maria and Gerda lived in the old farmhouse, on a farm now taken over by the common agricultural system of the country. Gerda worked on the communal farm and Maria worked in a dairy somewhere. I wondered vaguely why they were not working that day, but then I remembered that it was a Saturday.

Eventually the conversation came round to the means of our eventual departure or escape from the DDR. Meika and Gerda discussed the details. Apparently they knew somebody who owned a small boat and regularly transported people intent on leaving the DDR. The procedure was highly dangerous. A few people trying to escape in this way had been caught by the border patrols, but it appeared that the man in question had a good record of success. The person carrying out the transfer preferred to remain anonymous, the arrangements being made by somebody else. Gerda knew this other person and was willing to negotiate on behalf of Anna and me.

During the early evening Kurt left us to return to Berlin. This was necessary because of his job. Meika explained that she would stay at the farm for a few days, until the arrangements for our departure had been finalised.

After Kurt had gone, Meika and Gerda left on two ancient bicycles. 'We need to speak to Elsa, our contact, as soon as possible,' Gerda explained before they left. 'She will make the arrangements for us.'

Anna and I helped Maria wash the dishes while they were away. Maria understood very little English and she spoke German very rapidly, so Anna translated some of the conversation for me.

It was not long before Meika and Gerda returned, seemingly well pleased with their efforts.

'It's all been arranged,' announced Gerda. 'Elsa will contact the person who can take you to Denmark. We should hear within a few days whether he will do the job.'

Anna appeared to accept this. I was concerned about what would happen if the boatman did not want to take us. I had the impression that Meika and Gerda had not thought about that.

'What happens if he doesn't want to take the risk?' I asked.

Meika smiled. 'We have an alternative.' She directed her next few words to Gerda. 'There is also Captain Carlsen.'

The suggestion brought alarm to Maria. She shook her head as she spoke. 'Nein. Nein!' She reminded Gerda that he was unreliable, because he had allowed the last person he took to be arrested.

'But it was a complicated situation,' Gerda tried to point out.

Her comment did not pacify her mother, who pronounced emphatically, 'Man kann ihm nicht trauen.' [He cannot be trusted.]

'How many times has this Captain Carlsen transported people out of the country?' I asked.

'Several times,' Gerda replied. 'He has a ship that visits the DDR quite often.'

It seemed to me to be a precarious and highly dangerous situation. On the one hand Anna and I were dependent on an individual who might or might not agree to transport us across the sea to Denmark, and on the other we had someone whom Maria claimed was not to be trusted.

My thoughts were interrupted by Gerda. Her next question was directed at me. 'We will need some money. The price is 200 British pounds – or US dollars would be better. Have you got that amount of money?'

I shook my head. 'Not that much,' I replied. I took out the notes from my inside pocket and counted them. I had £170.

Gerda nodded. 'It is enough. We can find the rest.' She held out her hand for the money, which I gave her. It occurred to me that I was now penniless in the country.

I asked her whether the sum covered Anna as well as me.

She nodded. Anna made no comment. She had said very little to me since we had rescued her, and in most of the discussions that had taken place she had merely been an interested listener. I was determined to talk to her in private at the earliest opportunity.

In the meantime it now appeared that we would have to wait to see what our eventual route out of the country would be, if indeed there was to be one. Given the situation, it seemed that the undertaking was fraught with obstacles.

Chapter 15

It was two days before Anna and I heard of any further developments. In the meantime Meika had returned to Berlin and her job. On the Monday following our arrival Gerda and Maria had left the farmhouse early to go to work, leaving Anna and me on our own with strict instructions to keep out of sight and close to the house.

Since Anna's rescue from the apartment where she had been held captive, I had not had the opportunity to speak with her in private. There were so many questions I wanted to ask her, but the constant presence of other people made this impossible. I was looking forward to spending some time alone with her. I was also looking forward to having a proper rest. The sleeping arrangements in the farmhouse were not very good. Meika had been spending the night on the floor somewhere, and Anna was sharing a small bed with Gerda, while I was consigned to a rather hard sofa in the sitting room. I had not had a decent night's sleep since our arrival.

The morning turned out to be sunny and mild. After breakfast I was sitting in the living room reading an interesting book I had found, struggling with my limited German, when I suddenly realised that the house was very quiet. I wondered where Anna was, and I guessed that she was upstairs in the bedroom she was sharing with Gerda. Perhaps she too was in need of rest.

The fine weather beckoned me. I decided to wander out into the adjoining garden and large orchard, which appeared to be secluded from view. My first impression was how extensive this area was. The path meandered here and there between the fruit trees, which were already rich in blossom. The day was warm and I looked forward to sitting somewhere in the sunshine.

Rounding a corner, I spied Anna sitting on a bench. She looked sad and lonely. At first I wondered if she just wanted to be on her own, having found a little solitude. Her forlorn appearance changed my mind. I decided to try to talk to her.

She heard me approaching and glanced up. A hint of a smile accompanied her almost inaudible 'Hello'.

I sat down beside her, returning her greeting. There were a few seconds of silence between us.

'I'm very sorry about your sister,' I remarked softly.

She did not look at me or respond for a short time. When she did answer her voice was soft, almost as if she were talking to herself. 'I knew something would happen to her one day. I tried to warn her. I just did not think it would be like this – that she would be shot.'

'Would you like to tell me a bit more about her?' I asked.

Anna replied but still did not look up. 'She was friendly with people high up in power in both the American and the East German administrations. She gathered information from each side and then told it to the other.'

'Why did she do that?'

'I don't know. It became almost a way of life with her.'

'A very dangerous one,' I commented.

She nodded. 'Yes. I told her so, many times.'

'She had an apartment in East Berlin,' I remarked, remembering my efforts to contact Lena.

Anna looked at me briefly. 'She was a citizen of East Germany. She had an East German passport but she had a job that allowed her to travel to West Berlin quite frequently. Somehow, through the people she met, she also obtained a West German passport.'

'Tell me about you and Lena,' I suggested.

Anna directed her gaze at the ground in front of her and spoke again in a soft voice. 'Lena was my twin sister. We looked so much like each other that people could not tell us apart. When we were children, we liked playing games with the grown-up people, pretending to be each other.'

'And you were born in Poland?' I prompted.

Anna nodded. 'Yes. My mother is Polish. My father was from Germany. He died when my sister and I were only five years old. Then my mother met and married an officer in the Russian army and we moved to Berlin two years later.' She fell silent, I guessed remembering.

'What happened after that?' I asked softly.

She now appeared to be happy to continue relating her past life. 'Sergei, my mother's new husband, was not a very nice man. He drank heavily and beat my mother. He would also beat my sister and me just for small things. He made us learn Russian, and when we did not learn fast enough he called us lazy and he beat us for that as well.'

'That sounds awful,' I replied. 'What did your mother do about it?'

Anna gave a little sigh. 'There was not much she could do. He was a big man and she was very small. He also had other women. In the end our mother decided to leave him and return to Poland. That's when it all went wrong.'

'What do you mean?'

'At the last minute Sergei insisted that we girls remain with him; he manipulated the authorities so that they sided with him. My mother was heartbroken when she had to leave without us.'

I felt I needed to know more while Anna felt like talking. 'What happened after your mother left?' I asked.

Anna thought for a few moments. 'It was harder for Lena and me then. Sergei got a new woman to replace my mother and she was very strict with us.'

'Did you see your mother after that?'

'Not very often. She was too upset by everything. It changed her completely.'

'How long did you live with Sergei?'

We were ten when my mother left and I was sixteen when I left – about six years.'

I wanted to ask more questions, but Anna continued her story before I could say anything.

'Marika, the woman who moved into our house when our mother left, was sometimes not very nice to us. If we were naughty she would tell Sergei and he would beat us. Once they cut off all our hair as a punishment. I remember I cried a lot.'

'That was awful!' I exclaimed, shocked at the revelation.

'That was not all.' Anna now spoke almost in a whisper. 'Sergei and Marika used to have parties with Sergei's Russian friends. Lena and I sometimes had to sing or recite a piece of poetry in Russian for them as entertainment. I hated it.'

She paused again. 'Lena and I used to go to dancing classes. At one of the parties it was arranged that we would dance for everybody. At the last minute, they made us dance naked.' She stopped speaking and suddenly wiped a tear from her cheek.

Aghast, I asked, 'How old were you?'

'Eleven,' she whispered.

Compassion overwhelmed me. Suddenly I took her in my arms. 'It's all right now,' I said softly. She nestled into me and I held her for a few minutes, gently stroking her hair. Hearing her story helped me understand a great deal about her, but I knew there must be more.

'How did you eventually manage to leave that household and come to the west?' I asked her.

She replied immediately. 'At one of the parties, I became friendly with a young man who had a high position in government. I knew he travelled to West Berlin quite a lot and he knew I wanted to go there…' She paused for a second before continuing. 'He offered to smuggle me across the border in return for sleeping with him.'

'Did it work out?' I asked.

Anna nodded. 'Partly. I slept with him several times, and then he got me into West Berlin. It was not easy, but he knew ways of doing it, with a fake passport. I arrived, a refugee, in the west.'

'But you managed to settle in West Berlin?'

'Not at first. I discovered I was pregnant, and he abandoned me.'

Suddenly Anna raised herself from my shoulder. Almost for the first time she looked at me, her expression sad and enquiring. There were tears in her eyes. Her voice suddenly had more strength. 'So you see, I am not the innocent girl you might have thought I was.'

I held her close again. 'I like you just as you are,' I whispered and kissed her cheek. My lips tasted the tears that were trickling down her face.

Eventually I encouraged her to continue talking again. 'What happened after the man left you?' I asked quietly.

Anna sat up again and looked down at the ground. 'I lost the baby,' she explained simply.

'That must have been tough for you.'

Anna nodded. 'Yes, but I was fortunate. A lovely couple took me in and cared for me. They ran a religious group and were so kind and loving. It was something I had never experienced before. They helped me carry on with my life. I went to college, and I had a weekend job to try to pay for my keep.'

'That must have been a blessing.'

'It was. I don't know what would have happened to me if I hadn't met them.'

'What about Lena?' I asked next. 'How did she escape?'

Anna appeared to be more comfortable answering questions now. She replied quite readily. 'She married a young Russian army officer, one of the frequent visitors to Sergei and Marika's house. The marriage did not last long, but it enabled her to come to the west.'

I was about to ask another question, but Anna started to talk again.

'Unfortunately, she got involved in things that were not good for her. I tried to warn her, but she always said that what I had heard was just gossip.'

'Was she a spy?' After what Patrick had told me, I felt I had to ask.

Anna suddenly looked at me. 'Yes, I think at times she was. And look what happened to her. Shot for no reason at all.'

'Do you think it's true that she was shot trying to escape?'

She shrugged. 'Who knows? We will never find out the truth. I feel so sad and alone without her.'

As the memory flooded back to her, another tear ran down her cheek. She brushed it away quickly.

'I'm sorry you have lost your sister,' I said. I drew her close to me again and she nestled into my shoulder.

'We have to concentrate on leaving here now,' I whispered.

Anna did not move. 'Meika and Gerda make it sound easy, but it is not. The coastline is patrolled all the time. Many people have been caught. There is a strong possibility it will happen to us.'

'No. It won't happen,' I asserted. Even as I refuted the suggestion, I knew there was truth in what she was saying.

She spoke again. 'If we are caught, it will be bad for me. I am Lena's sister. I will spend years in prison. The prisons in the DDR are not nice places.'

I tried to reassure her. 'It won't happen.'

She shook her head. 'You will be all right. You are English. They will have to release you.'

I knew that escaping from East Germany was dangerous. Some of the people who had been caught attempting it had been shot by the border guards. It seemed odd that within the last few days I had become a person on the run. My attempt to find Anna had been successful, but the result had not been what I expected.

Anna broke the temporary silence between us. Quite out of the blue she looked at me and forced a brief smile. 'I would like to make some coffee. Will you have a cup?'

'Good idea.'

She reached under the bench and pulled out what turned out to be a pair of Gerda's shoes. They were old and tatty but serviceable. We both stood up. The sun had now retreated behind some clouds and a chilly wind was blowing.

We walked back to the farmhouse in silence, and at one point Anna placed her hand in mine.

Back in the kitchen she busied herself producing two mugs of coffee, which she placed on the table in front of us. No words had passed between us since we left the garden, but I was once again eager to hear more about her past life, in particular how she had taken up with Boris.

I broke the silence. 'How did you meet Boris Smirnov and come to England?'

Anna clasped her hands around her mug of coffee. She gazed down at the table as she replied. 'I was approached by the Americans. They wanted to know more about him. They did not trust him. They knew that Lena and I looked very alike. The American security service contacted me and told me that if I made contact with Boris and had an affair with him, they would ensure that Lena would be kept safe.'

She looked at me and then spoke again. 'So you see, I kept my promise but they did not keep theirs. My sister is dead.'

Tears started to appear once again in her eyes. I reached over and took her hand. 'Tell me about you and Boris,' I suggested.

Anna wiped her tears away. 'It was easy enough for me to make contact with him and pretend to be Lena. I had done it many times before in other situations. Boris was immediately attracted to me and almost at once asked me to go to England with him.'

She hesitated for a few seconds. When she spoke again it was in a quiet voice. 'It was all right at first, but then it all changed. Perhaps he became suspicious. I don't know. But he changed. He made me stay in the house and he treated me very badly. He told me that if I tried to run away he would tell the police and he would make sure that I went to prison. That frightened me.'

Anna's revelations made things a bit clearer. She had certainly had quite a hard life and had been abused by a lot of people. Listening to her relating her experiences increased my sympathy and admiration for her. As for Boris, I already had a poor opinion of him, but his treatment of Anna had been diabolical.

'I'm sorry you had such a bad time with him,' I said.

Anna went quiet, perhaps remembering past events. There was one thing I felt I should tell her, but I hesitated to bring up the subject. In the end my curiosity overcame my reluctance to admit my guilt. I tried to ask my question in the best way to avoid causing her any offence or embarrassment.

I cleared my throat. 'I have something to confess to you, but at the same time I am a bit puzzled.'

Anna looked at me enquiringly.

'When I decided to come to Berlin to look for you, I am afraid I had to go through some of your personal possessions. I was surprised to find your sister's passport as well as yours.'

Before she could react, I rushed in with an apology. 'I'm sorry I had to do that, but I was looking for information that might help me find you.'

'It does not matter,' Anna murmured. 'The passport with Lena's name is a forgery. She obtained it for me. She had contacts who could do that sort of thing.'

'That explains a lot,' I replied.

Anna nodded. She was about to say something else when there was a noise outside. The door opened and Gerda and

Maria entered. Gerda was smiling broadly. We hardly had time to respond to their greeting when Gerda made an announcement.

'It's all fixed. You will be picked up tonight and taken to Denmark.'

Chapter 16

Gerda was clearly excited. She sat down at the table and explained in more detail. 'We will need to be on the beach at midnight or just before. The boat will come in close to the shore and you will have to go out to it.'

'What sort of boat will it be?' I asked.

'It is small. A dinghy, I think it is called.'

'But there are border patrols,' broke in Anna.

Gerda nodded. 'Yes, that is a problem, trying to evade the patrol boats. But the owner of the dinghy has made the crossing several times. He knows the area well and he is good at it.'

Neither Anna nor I made any comment. I knew Anna was apprehensive and I did not relish the thought of trying to play cat and mouse with the DDR, who were clearly doing their best to stop any activities they did not approve of taking place along the coastline. But it seemed that there was little alternative other than to take the risk. If we attempted to cross using an official route, it was certain that we would both be arrested. For me that would perhaps mean a few difficult days, but for Anna the situation would be different – it could mean months or even years in an East German prison.

Gerda continued to outline the plan as she helped Maria prepare a meal. 'We will have to leave here in good time, as it will take us an hour to walk to the pickup point. It is on an isolated part of the coast. At least it will be a dark night, which is ideal.'

This gave me a measure of reassurance, but I could tell from Anna's face that she was very anxious about the whole thing.

While we were eating, Gerda told us a bit about her life. She explained that she had wanted to be a nurse when she left school, but at the time there were no vacancies and she had been directed into farming. She quite enjoyed the physical work, but she wished the wall would come down and that she could travel to the west.

I asked her where she would like to go and she said she wanted to visit her cousins in America. 'One day, perhaps,' she sighed.

The next few hours were tinged with excitement and apprehension as we waited to embark on the hazardous journey. Gerda and Maria continued chatting in an attempt to keep our minds off the task ahead. Maria kept offering us more and more food, insisting that we would not have a chance to eat anything for many hours, but neither of us felt very hungry.

It was coming up to eleven when Gerda got up from her seat and announced that it was time to leave. Apparently we had to walk a mile or so to the seashore. Anna and I had few possessions and were obliged to travel in the clothes we had arrived in, although Gerda had found a better pair of shoes for Anna and a warm jacket for her to wear. At the last minute, Maria eyed me up and produced an old jacket for me, which though a little large provided an extra layer of warmth.

After extending our gratitude and thanks to Maria, we set out, Gerda leading the way. It appeared that for the most part we would be walking over fields and at times rough tracks. The night was dark and in places it was impossible to miss areas of mud from recent rain. Occasionally we slipped on the hazardous surface and once I narrowly missed ending up full length on the ground. For Anna it was even more difficult. The shoes Gerda had given her had a slight heel, which tended to stick in the mud on the path. On more than one occasion she left a shoe behind and I retrieved it from the sticky mess while she balanced on one foot. We were all relieved when the surface became firmer.

After a while we could hear the sound of waves breaking and we found ourselves climbing steep sand dunes. Suddenly the ocean lay before us, with only a short strip of sand separating us from the water.

'This is the place,' Gerda whispered. 'We have to wait here.'

I looked at my watch and could just about make out that it was about twenty minutes short of midnight. Anna found a clump of grass and sat down and tried to clean the mud off her shoes. I followed her example. Gerda remained standing, always alert.

We waited in the darkness, for the most part unable to make out any movement on the dark expanse of sea. Abruptly we became aware of the sound of a boat engine, and the next instant the area was lit up by a powerful searchlight. Gerda immediately crouched down behind a sand dune, and Anna and I quickly followed suit.

It took half a minute or so for the boat and its searchlight to disappear. Gerda resumed her former position, peering into the darkness for signs of the dinghy.

'That was the border patrol boat,' she announced quietly, dusting sand off her clothes.

We continued to wait, aware that the patrol boat would be returning soon. Eventually Gerda broke the silence. She attempted to look at her watch as she spoke. 'Paul should have been here by now. He has to come to the beach, pick you up and then be out of sight before the patrol boat returns ten minutes from now.'

I could sense and understand Gerda's concern. It was a narrow window of time in which to make any undetected movement in between the patrols. I was intrigued that this was the first time Gerda had named our potential rescuer.

The patrol boat returned. This time it was closer to the shore and its searchlight swept along the beach and the dunes where we were hiding. The three of us flung ourselves completely flat on the ground as we waited for it to move on.

The light disappeared and we all sat up and dusted off our clothes.

This occurred again and again. The patrol boat would appear, sweep the area with its searchlight, disappear for about ten minutes and then reappear. Gerda was by now clearly becoming quite concerned. She looked at her watch after each visit by the boat. I peered at mine. The hands now showed half past twelve. We had been waiting for nearly an hour. A cool wind was sweeping in from the sea, giving the night a chilly feel.

Anna raised a further concern. 'It's getting quite windy. Will that stop the boat coming?'

'It's not too strong yet,' Gerda replied, still gazing intently out to sea, though it was almost impossible to see anything in the darkness.

Despite Gerda's reassurance, I was beginning to feel apprehensive about travelling to Denmark in a small open boat with a breeze blowing that appeared to be gathering strength.

'Something must have happened,' Gerda announced anxiously. 'Paul is always on time.'

'Will he come on another night?' Anna asked.

'I don't know.'

I made no comment. I could see that Gerda was now very worried and Anna was becoming quite stressed. Waiting there close to the beach did not improve the situation. At regular intervals the patrol boat appeared on its monotonous journey up and down the coast, its searchlight illuminating the area as it passed. It was a constant reminder of the passing of the time.

Eventually Gerda looked at her watch one last time, which prompted me to look at mine. The hands showed that it was now after one o'clock.

Gerda shook her head. 'He will not come now. It is too late. We have to go back.'

She started to make her way back through the dunes. Despondently, Anna and I joined her. Our bid to escape had clearly failed.

There was little conversation between us as we walked back. We were each lost in our own thoughts. I found the return journey long and tedious, once again having to negotiate the muddy ground. It was with some relief that we arrived back at the farmhouse. We deposited our shoes outside and entered the warm and welcoming atmosphere of the kitchen, which Gerda plunged into light as her hand found the light switch. We were alone. Clearly Maria had long since gone to bed.

'I will make a drink for us,' Gerda announced.

It took her several minutes to boil a kettle of water and produce a herbal tea. We all sat round the table.

'What will happen to us now?' asked Anna.

'When I go to work, I will be able to find out more,' replied Gerda. 'Elsa works with me.'

'What happens if Paul is unable to take us?' I asked.

'We will have to find an alternative.'

'Is that possible?' I asked. Previous conversations had seemed to indicate that Captain Carlsen, Gerda's earlier suggestion, would be extremely unreliable.

Gerda appeared to be deep in thought. 'It may take some time,' she replied.

'Perhaps we should just give ourselves up,' Anna murmured quietly.

Gerda was aghast. 'What? No! You can't do that.'

Her reaction did not appear to have any effect on Anna, who sat gazing down at the table, her hands clasped around a mug. She looked up at me and spoke again in the same quiet voice. 'Lena is dead. Now they want me. They will not arrest you. They will just tell you off for being late returning to the barrier.' There were tears in her eyes.

Her suggestion had come as a bit of a shock to me. I reacted swiftly, placing my hand on her arm as I spoke. 'No. We are leaving together and returning to England. Giving ourselves up is not an option.'

Anna did not reply. She returned her gaze to the table and took a sip of her drink. I wondered what had prompted her suggestion.

It was Gerda who changed the mood of our little group. 'Look, let us not consider alternatives at present. We don't know what has happed to Paul. Perhaps his boat broke down. It is difficult to get things fixed here. Tomorrow I will find out what happened.'

As she spoke she stood up and took her mug over to the sink. It was the signal for all of us to try to get some sleep. The clock on the wall indicated three o'clock and I knew that Gerda left for work at around six. She was going to be tired in the morning.

Anna quietly left the room with the words, 'I will go to sleep now. Gute Nacht.'

Gerda quickly followed. I lay down on the couch, but sleep would not come. There was too much to think about. I wondered why Paul had not turned up and what would happen to us now. I was reluctant to put my life in the hands of Captain Carlsen, but no other alternative seemed to be available. I was also disturbed and puzzled by Anna's suggestion that we give ourselves up. I knew that I had to talk to her again at the earliest possible moment.

Chapter 17

I awoke the next morning after a very short and disturbed night. The events of the previous day remained uppermost in my mind. I seemed to have been plunged into a strange and unreal world. I could hear movement in the kitchen and guessed that Gerda was preparing some breakfast for her mother and herself.

I lay there for a short time and then decided that I might as well get up and start the day, whatever that might bring. After visiting the bathroom, I wandered into the kitchen, where Gerda and Maria were having breakfast. When our morning greetings were over, Gerda wanted to get me something to eat, but I declined her offer, knowing that she and Maria had to leave for work shortly. I helped myself to some coffee.

It was not long before Anna joined us. She looked pale and sad. She poured herself a mug of coffee and sat quietly at the table. There was very little conversation between us all.

Eventually Gerda looked at the clock and jumped up. 'We have to go to work,' she announced. Maria also made a move, and they left on their ancient bicycles with the usual courtesies, Gerda assuring us that she would find out what had happened to Paul and our failed transportation.

Anna and I were left alone at the kitchen table, slowly sipping our coffee. It was the opportunity I had been waiting for.

It was Anna who spoke first, her eyes fixed on the mug she was holding. 'You must think very badly of me.'

Her statement caught me unawares, but I knew that it reflected the aura of sadness that surrounded her. I responded quickly. 'Think badly of you? Why should I do that?'

She took a few seconds to answer. 'I was not honest with you. I deceived you.'

'What do you mean?'

Anna's eyes met mine. 'When I came to you, you thought I was Lena, and—'

'But you explained all that,' I interrupted.

She shook her head. 'I deceived you. It was not the right thing to do.'

I was about to make a further comment, but she continued to speak, her gaze again fixed on the mug. 'Boris treated me very badly. At first it was not so bad, but after a while he was very cruel to me.'

'Was that after he got another girlfriend?' I asked.

She nodded. 'Yes, I think so.'

'It was a pity you couldn't have left him.'

Anna took another sip of coffee. 'It is true that he threatened to report me if I tried to leave, but I also stayed because of my agreement with the Americans, to try to protect Lena.'

She paused for a second and then spoke more quietly. 'But it was no good. Lena is dead, after all I went through.'

I could see tears forming in her eyes. I reached out and touched her hand. 'I'm sorry,' I whispered.

She appeared to want to continue talking. 'Towards the end it was horrible living with Boris. I would have done anything to get away from him.' She paused. 'And then you appeared.'

'Did you want to come and stay with me?' I queried.

'At first I just wanted to get away from Boris, but I liked you from the start.'

'And then?' I prompted.

Anna looked up at me again. There were still tears in her eyes. 'I came to you. You were so kind to me. You were so caring and loving. It was something I had never experienced from a man before.'

'It was my pleasure,' I replied.

'But I was not honest with you, and I cannot forgive myself for that. There were times I wanted to tell you the truth, but always it seemed easier to just let things continue as they were. I wanted to remain feeling safe and happy and to have fun.'

I tried to find the words to reassure her, but 'I understand' was all I could manage.

Now that we were talking at last, I was keen to learn more about what had happened to Anna. 'Why were you kidnapped from my house?' I asked.

She was quick to answer. 'That was arranged by Max Meyer.'

'But why?'

'He hoped that through me he could find out where Lena was.'

'But why was he so anxious to find Lena?'

Anna seemed to be thinking carefully before answering. 'He has always had a special relationship with people in high positions in the East German government, but recently that relationship has not been so good. If he had produced Lena, it would have restored his position of favour.'

'Gosh, that's almost unbelievable.' I was amazed that such things could happen.

One aspect of the story was still puzzling me. 'How did Max Meyer know where you were?'

Anna shrugged. 'Who knows? These people have spies everywhere.' She thought for a few seconds and then added, 'Perhaps Boris told him. I think towards the end of my stay with him he knew he had been fooled and that I was not Lena.'

She was silent for a short time, perhaps remembering.

'What happened to you after you were taken from my house?' I asked.

'I don't remember much. They drugged me most of the time. I remember that we went on a ship and then by car, and then they left me in that awful apartment with that horrible couple.'

I could see that she was close to tears again. I reached out and took her hand. 'Tell me more,' I urged in a soft voice.

'They chained me up like a dog, and…' She looked at me, tears appearing again as she spoke. 'They tried to make me tell them where Lena was. They did not believe me when I kept telling them I did not know, and they tried many things to get me to speak. Then they became violent with me. Once they stripped me naked and tied my hands and feet and put me in a bath of cold water. I screamed and screamed. In the end they had to lift me out.'

'How awful!' I exclaimed.

'You rescued me just in time. They told me all the things they were going to do to me if I didn't tell them where Lena was. They would not believe me.' As she finished speaking, she brushed a tear from her cheek.

I leaned across the table towards her, still holding her hand. 'It's all over now,' I whispered. She became quiet again.

I still had more questions. 'How well do you know this Max Meyer?'

'He was a friend of Sergei's and he often came to the house when Lena and I lived with Sergei and Marika.' She paused and looked at me. 'He tried to rape me once. I scratched his face. He has never forgiven me.'

The ups and downs of Anna's previous life amazed me. She had experienced so much, yet she had survived.

I asked her another question. 'What would have happened to you when Max Meyer found out that Lena was dead if we hadn't managed to get you away from the apartment?'

'He could have killed me. He is quite capable of that. Or he might have handed me over to the Stasi and told them lies about me.'

'It's a good thing we got to you when we did,' I replied.

'But now we are in a worse situation.'

'What do you mean?'

'It's only a matter of time before we are arrested.' There was sadness in her voice.

I responded quickly. 'No. It isn't like that. We are going to get away and you are coming back to England with me.'

Anna shook her head. 'No. We will be arrested. I feel it. I know it.'

'But we don't yet know what happened last night – why Paul didn't turn up,' I pointed out.

Anna was not convinced. She repeated what she had said to me previously. 'It is very dangerous, what we are trying to do. Many people have failed. We will be caught and arrested. You are a British citizen, and they will have to release you, but I will go to prison, perhaps for many years. The prisons in East Germany are not nice places.'

'But some people do make it to freedom. We could be two of them.'

Anna did not appear to be convinced. She was silent for a minute or two, deep in thought. Then she spoke again, almost to herself.

'I should give myself up. I have caused all this trouble for everybody.'

I was again horrified at the suggestion. I reacted quickly. 'No! You cannot do that. It would be madness and you would be letting the people down who are trying to help us – good people like Gerda and Maria.'

Anna said nothing, and I again returned to persuasion. 'You must not think of doing that. Promise me you won't do it.'

She did not reply, but simply nodded briefly. She stood up, picked up our empty mugs, took them to the sink and ran some water to wash them up. I felt that she understood the point I was making and I decided to let the conversation end there. It was now best to wait and see what Gerda would find out about what happened last night.

Anna turned from the sink and looked at me. She was trying to smile. 'How about some breakfast?' she asked.

While we had been talking, I had not thought about food. Anna's suggestion appealed to me immensely. 'Good idea,' I responded with enthusiasm.

'I will get some for us,' she replied.

It was late in the afternoon when Gerda and Maria returned. I could see at once that they were not the bearers of good news. Gerda looked glum as she sat down facing Anna and me. She addressed us in German.

'Paul was arrested last night.'

Anna clasped her hand to her mouth. 'Oh, no! I knew it would go wrong.'

'What will happen now?' I asked.

Gerda responded immediately. 'We cannot use that route any more. It is too dangerous. The border control will be watching. We will have to consider Captain Carlsen.'

The suggestion brought immediate concern from Maria. 'Captain Carlsen is not to be trusted.'

'You told us that he is not reliable,' added Anna.

'He has been useful in the past,' Gerda replied.

'Can you tell us a bit more about him?' I asked.

Gerda was happy to explain. 'He has a small ship and he transports goods between here and Poland, but occasionally he visits Denmark.'

I needed to know more. 'What about this suggestion about him not being reliable? I asked.

'I told you – he had someone arrested who was trying to escape. He is not to be trusted,' retorted Maria.

'But we don't know what really happened,' Gerda pointed out.

This did not appear to convince her mother, who again muttered that Captain Carlsen was not to be trusted.

'He is our only hope,' Gerda explained.

'We will all be arrested,' insisted Maria, gloomily.

'We don't know what really happened when the person was arrested,' Gerda insisted. 'He had succeeded in smuggling several people to Denmark before that.'

It was clear that Gerda and her mother held different opinions as to the reliability of this Captain Carlsen. Depending on him certainly did not seem like a very good means of escape to me.

I asked, 'Has he carried out any successful escapes since the arrest of that person?'

'We aren't sure. We think he has,' replied Gerda.

Something else occurred to me. I had given all my English money to Gerda to pay for our transportation. Presumably with the arrest of Paul this had now been lost.

I thought I had better raise this with our hosts. 'What will have happened to the money for our escape now that Paul has been arrested?' I added hurriedly, 'It was all I had.'

Gerda smiled. 'It was collected from the pickup point as arranged, but don't worry. We can handle that problem. You can pay us back later.'

It now seemed clear to me that Gerda and her mother were more deeply involved in escapes from East Germany than I had at first imagined.

It was Maria who broke up the conversation, announcing that she was going to prepare something to eat. She turned her attention to the stove. Gerda immediately jumped up and started to help her. Anna offered to assist them, and I was left to my own thoughts.

It seemed that Anna and I were now in a very precarious situation. One avenue for escape was now clearly closed to us, and the only alternative seemed questionable. I prayed that Anna would not give any more thought to handing herself over to the East German authorities.

All things considered, it was not a hopeful place to be in.

Chapter 18

It was several days before we had any information about what would happen next. In the meantime Anna and I remained at the farmhouse. A kind of routine set in. Each day Maria and Gerda would depart for work, leaving us to amuse ourselves as best we could. I tended to read quite a lot, improving my German from the supply of books in the house. Anna did odd bits of housework in an endeavour to help Maria and Gerda. Sometimes she would relate further snippets about how her life had been before we met, and she would ask me about mine. It all seemed quite cosy, but over us hung the realisation that our escape from East Germany was in the balance. It appeared that Gerda's contact was waiting for the return of Captain Carlsen and his ship before anything more could happen.

One little highlight was an unexpected visit from Karl and Meika, who had been shocked and concerned when they learned of our failed escape. There was much discussion between Meika, Gerda and Maria about our situation and what to do next. Unfortunately, Anna and I felt that we could add little to the conversation, due to our lack of knowledge.

Meika and Karl stayed for an evening meal and then had to drive back to Berlin. Before they left, they wished us luck in securing our escape safely and quickly.

Four days after our failed attempt to leave, Gerda arrived home looking quite cheerful. 'The police have released Paul,' she announced with a smile.

This was welcome news. It had been sobering to realise that Paul had been arrested while trying to assist us.

'What happened?' I asked.

'It seems they didn't have enough evidence to keep him any longer,' Gerda replied.

'I am so pleased,' said Anna.

Gerda had more to tell us. 'Elsa thinks that Captain Carlsen's ship will be returning this week. She will talk to him about taking you to Denmark.'

'But he is not reliable. He might turn us over to the police,' Anna protested, looking anxious.

'How can we trust him, after what has happened in the past?' I asked.

'He is not to be trusted,' insisted Maria.

Gerda did her best to reassure us. 'Elsa feels it is all right to trust him. She knows him quite well and I have confidence in what she says.'

Realising that perhaps we still required convincing, Gerda added a bit more. 'He has transported several people to safety. There are questions hanging over the one time when he failed. Everything is in favour of trusting him. He is the only opportunity we have now.'

'He will let you down,' muttered Maria.

I suddenly thought of something that might help. 'Will we be able to meet him beforehand?' I asked.

'I can ask Elsa to arrange that,' replied Gerda.

'Perhaps it would be advisable to make a decision after we have spoken to him, then,' I suggested.

Gerda readily agreed. 'Yes. I think that would be a very good idea.'

My suggestion seemed to offer some sort of solution to the problem. There was no other option on the table. At least if we were able to talk to this possible saviour, we might then have enough information to decide whether to take the risk of travelling with him. Gerda agreed to discuss the matter further with Elsa, who would then arrange a meeting with Captain Carlsen.

For a few days there was no further word about the plan. For Anna and me, life was beginning to get boring, there being little to do each day other than read, talk or do odd jobs as best we could. It was on one of these days, a bright sunny one, that we took our mugs of coffee out into the garden and sat on our favourite bench enjoying the warmth of the sun. Anna was wearing a short-sleeved blouse given to her by Gerda, which clearly revealed the tiny tattoo on her upper arm. I had always wondered how she came about it.

'How did you get that?' I asked, indicating the mark.

At first Anna appeared still to be reluctant to offer any explanation; she glanced at the tattoo and then made the same reply as before. 'It was done a long time ago.'

I was determined to press for more information. 'Did you ask to have it done?' I asked.

Anna hesitated for a second, and then shook her head slowly. 'No,' she replied simply.

It was clear that there was an unpleasant story connected with the tattoo. I decided it was best to be kind and not ask any more questions. Perhaps in time she would tell me. I was surprised when she started to speak once more.

'It was a long time ago, when Lena and I were with Sergei and Marika. We were just fourteen years old. Sergei used to get angry when we played games and he did not know which was me and which was Lena. One day he and Marika took us out in the car. We did not know where we were going.'

She stopped talking for a second, clearly reliving the event. There were tears in her eyes. I placed a hand on her shoulder. She continued to speak quietly.

'They took us to a place where they did tattoos. At first I did not understand what it was all about, but then they made me sit in a chair. There was a man with some sort of equipment. I knew that something horrible was going to happen, and I screamed and struggled.'

She stopped.

'And?' I prompted.

'They told me that if I did not behave they would tie me to the chair and it would be done anyway.'

'Who did?' I asked.

'Sergei and Marika. They were determined to do it.'

She sighed. 'Then the man did this to me.' She glanced at the tattoo again.

I put my arm around her. She leaned in towards me and buried her head in my shoulder. Her voice was slightly muffled as she continued speaking. 'Then they did the same to Lena.'

'I'm sorry you had to go through that,' I whispered.

Anna remained silent. I gently stroked her hair as she rested against me. My admiration for her had increased considerably since she had told me about her unhappy childhood. She had had a horrific early life with many challenges, yet she had survived by sheer determination. I knew now that I had fallen deeply in love with her and now only wanted to get us out of our present predicament and return with her to the UK.

When Gerda came back from work that afternoon, we learned that there had been a new development.

'Captain Carlsen's ship is back in port!' she announced excitedly. 'Elsa has arranged for you to meet him at her house this evening. We will go there after we have eaten.'

At last we had some good news. Even Anna seemed to brighten up at the prospect of meeting Captain Carlsen, and as a result our evening meal was a more cheerful event than usual.

A little later we set out to walk the three miles to Gerda's contact's house by the coast, as Gerda and Maria did not own a car. Most of our way was along tracks in between fields. Fortunately the route was not as muddy as the one we had followed a few nights previously.

As we approached the settlement, it became clear that it was little more than a village, with just a few houses, a church, some warehouses and a small quay. We started to walk past the warehouses. It was extremely quiet. We did not see anyone, although at one point Gerda, on hearing a noise, motioned us to take cover beside one of the buildings. What had alarmed her turned out to be a man on a bicycle, who went on his way without noticing us.

Shortly afterwards we came to a group of houses. Gerda led us up to one of them and tapped on the door.

After a few seconds the door was opened by a middle-aged woman with blonde hair, who quickly ushered us into a large kitchen.

Gerda introduced the woman as Elsa, who seemed quite friendly and immediately offered us a glass of wine. Sitting at the kitchen table, sipping the wine, I began to feel quite relaxed. Elsa informed us that Captain Carlsen would arrive soon.

We chatted for about ten minutes. Then came a knock at the door. Elsa rushed to open it. The man who stood there smiling was clearly Captain Carlsen. He was tall, and was wearing a sailor's jersey and a traditional sailor's cap. I guessed he was aged around forty. He was carrying a bundle under each arm. After he had gone around shaking hands and greeting each of us, Gerda ushered him to a seat and Elsa produced a glass of wine for him. There was little conversation. All our eyes were on him.

From his position at the head of the table, he cast his eye over Anna and me. He addressed us slowly in a strong accent. 'You wish that I take you to Denmark?'

There was a moment of silence around the table while he waited for a response. I felt that it was up to me to say something. 'We want to know whether we can reach Denmark safely,' I remarked.

After another few seconds of silence, Captain Carlsen appeared to almost frown as he replied. 'It is always dangerous, but I will do my best to get you there safely.'

Everybody was looking at me. It was decision time and it appeared that what happened was to come from me. I knew we were taking a risk, but what Captain Carlsen was offering seemed now to be the only route to escape. I looked at Anna. With a look of resignation on her face, she gave a slight nod of agreement.

I turned to Captain Carlsen again. 'We would like you to take us to Denmark.'

He nodded his assent.

At this point Gerda produced an envelope full of banknotes and handed it to him. As well as English notes I spotted some American dollars.

Captain Carlsen carefully counted the notes. I noted that the amount was in excess of what I had given Gerda. Clearly, if we escaped, I owed somebody some money.

Captain Carlsen again nodded his agreement as he slowly and carefully stowed the money away in one of his pockets. He sipped his wine in silence.

We all waited for his instructions. They were not long in coming. He spoke again in his slow voice. 'Tomorrow at midnight you come to my ship.'

There was a pause. Then he asked, 'Can you swim?'

That was unexpected, and a bit of a shock. Fortunately, at university I had been quite a good swimmer over moderate distances. I replied with a simple 'Yes'.

I turned to Anna. 'How about you?'

'At school I was top of my class in swimming.'

Our replies were received with another nod and a brief 'Good' from Captain Carlsen.

'How far will we have to swim?' I asked.

'My ship, the *Carl Lodeson*, will be anchored about thirty metres offshore,' he replied. 'I will put a rope ladder in place for you to climb up. You will have to avoid being caught by the searchlight.'

This seemed to be quite straightforward, although the thought of having to swim out to the ship in the dark appeared daunting and, I thought, unnecessary. I was certainly not prepared for his next remarks.

'I have brought these for you to wear when you are swimming.' He indicated the two bundles he had brought with him. 'I need to have dry clothes from you for you to wear on the ship.'

This came as a shock. The only clothes we had with us were the ones we were wearing. I could see at once the alarm on Anna's face. Captain Carlsen's remark immediately prompted discussion between Gerda and Elsa. Their solution was not one I favoured. We were to change into the garments Captain Carlsen had brought with him and hand over the clothes we were wearing. Anna and I were not at all enthusiastic. It seemed odd to me that we had not been warned in advance, particularly as Gerda and Elsa had clearly done all this before. More discussion followed, but in the end it became clear that this was our only option.

Things were happening really quickly, and it now appeared to be the general opinion that we should accept Captain Carlsen's offer of transportation and comply with his request.

Anna and I found ourselves being ushered into another room, each carrying one of the bundles. We lost no time in discovering what we had been given to wear. All that was in each bundle was a single garment, a boiler suit. Anna held hers up and made a face. I was surprised at her next move: she quickly stripped down to her underwear. I followed suit. Keeping my underpants on I stepped into the boiler suit. Clearly our underwear was going to get wet, but that was a problem for later. The boiler suit fitted me well enough. The same could not be said for Anna. The garment was much too big for her. I remembered to remove my passport and a few other personal items from my clothing and transfer them to the pockets of the boiler suit. I made a mental note to enclose them in some sort of waterproof protection before we went into the water.

Having donned our escape garb, we returned to the kitchen. In the brighter light of the kitchen, the garments Anna and I were wearing appeared to be odd and quite out of keeping with our situation. We both felt we looked ridiculous and now suffered some embarrassment. Gerda and Elsa set about trying to rectify the problems with Anna's boiler suit. They chopped about a foot off each leg and provided her with a belt to bunch up the ample waste. We were both now barefoot. An old pair of shoes was found for Anna, which were about two sizes too big for her, and I was given an old pair of boots that were slightly too small – but at least we had some footwear for the present.

We dumped our own clothes on the table, and Gerda and Elsa immediately started to tie them up into two bundles for Captain Carlsen to take away. I was impressed to see that they managed to pack them down quite small. Captain Carlsen looked on but made no comment, occasionally sipping his wine and puffing on a rather disagreeable pipe.

As soon as the bundles were ready, Captain Carlsen prepared to leave. He looked at Anna and me. 'I see you tomorrow night. Midnight. No later.' With a brief handshake all round, he took his leave, our clothing under his arm.

We took our leave of Elsa and made our way back to the farmhouse in silence, Anna and I both conscious of our somewhat inadequate clothing. A fresh breeze had sprung up and I certainly felt the chill, and I saw Anna shiver several times. Once or twice she walked right out of the shoes she was wearing. We were glad to arrive back at our base.

There was little talk before we turned in for the night. My thoughts were on the following night and how we would fare. Though the arrangements were in place, there still seemed to be a lot of uncertainty. Watching Captain Carlsen walk away with all the respectable clothes we possessed, I had begun to ponder on what might happen before we were reunited with them. The captain was an unknown quantity. Most certainly he was a man of few words, and this added to the anxiety I was feeling.

As I lay on the hard couch, I could not help wondering whether our mission would be successful, and if it was not, what would happen to us. Anna's foreboding of failure after our previous attempt to escape came back to haunt me. Was this going to be the outcome of all our efforts? The element of uncertainty was now very real and I realised how fragile our position was. Tomorrow we were going to have to put all our trust in Captain Carlsen.

Chapter 19

The next day was an anxious one for us. Once Gerda and Maria had gone off to work, Anna and I were left to our leisure and our thoughts. After washing up the various dishes from breakfast, Anna announced that she wanted to wash her hair and disappeared into the bathroom.

Left on my own, I tried to take my mind off what was ahead of us and occupied my time by reading. Several hours passed before Anna reappeared. She entered the kitchen silently, having abandoned the socks she had been given by Gerda. She moved towards me, and I could see at once that she needed my help. I stood up and put my arm round her.

She snuggled into me and whispered, 'Hold me. I am frightened.'

'What are you frightened about?' I whispered in return.

'We will be arrested tonight. I feel it. I know it.'

Despite my own concerns, I knew I had to try to provide some sort of comfort and reassurance. 'Everything has been arranged. Once we are on the ship we will be safe.'

Anna shook her head. 'I do not trust Captain Carlsen,' she murmured.

'I'm sure it will be all right.' I tried to appear confident, but I knew my words were having little effect on how she was feeling.

My thoughts were confirmed by her next comment. 'It's horrible being in prison in the DDR.' She hesitated. 'They arrested me once at the border.'

This disclosure alarmed me. 'What for?' I asked.

Her head buried in my shoulder, she explained. 'It was one time when I had visited my mother. I had some food I had brought with me. They accused me of stealing from the DDR and arrested me.'

'What happened?' I asked softly.

'They kept me for two days in prison and then let me go.'

'That must have been a horrible experience.'

'Yes. It was awful.'

Suddenly she raised her head and looked at me. Tears were forming in her eyes. 'They stripped me naked and searched me – everywhere. I thought I was going to die.'

'It won't happen this time.'

She did not reply. I stroked her hair gently and continued to hold her. Despite my efforts to reassure her that all would be well, I had my own reservations about the ordeal ahead of us. It seemed that we were in a position where we had no personal control and were obliged to put our trust in someone who apparently had a dubious record. We were very much in the hands of third parties.

When Gerda and Maria returned from work, their chat about various other topics as we ate our evening meal lifted somewhat the gloom that both Anna and I were feeling. Despite my best efforts, Anna remained apprehensive and fearful, more or less convinced that our attempt to gain freedom would end in disaster.

It was past ten o'clock when Gerda announced that it was time for us to leave. Our preparations were brief, as we had nothing to take with us. All that Anna and I had to do was to change into the boiler suits and put on footwear. After that we took our final leave of Maria and thanked her for keeping us safe over the previous few days. She seemed sad to see us go and appeared to be almost tearful.

Grateful for the hospitality that Maria and Gerda had provided us with, I made a mental note that if our bid to escape was successful and we managed to make it back to England, I would have to make things up to them in some way.

Once outside, we again felt the chill of the night in our inadequate clothing, even though Gerda had lent us each a coat to wear on the journey. The moon, which had brightened the sky earlier, had disappeared behind clouds. Unable to see the path, on several occasions we strayed off course and stepped onto uneven ground. For Anna walking was particularly difficult because her shoes kept slipping off.

Eventually we arrived at Elsa's house. She must have been watching for our approach, because she opened the door before we had a chance to knock. She was already dressed to go out. Exchanges were brief, as she immediately indicated that we needed to leave without delay.

We followed her in silence through the streets. Fortunately there did not appear to be anybody around, so our progress was not impeded in any way. It did not take long for us to reach the harbour, which in the gloom seemed to consist of little more than a small quay that was littered with coal debris presumably left over from deliveries by sea. Several ships lay at anchor off the shore, and in the poor light it was impossible for us to make out which was the *Carl Lodeson*. Elsa, however, was well informed and she quickly pointed out a small vessel anchored some distance away. We moved through the shadows closer to our goal. I was concerned that the ship appeared to be further away from land than the thirty metres Captain Carlsen had mentioned.

Suddenly we became aware of a searchlight scouring the shoreline. Elsa reacted immediately, ushering us into the cover of a nearby building. After a few agonising seconds the brilliant light had moved on.

As we emerged from our concealment, Elsa turned to us. 'You have to avoid being caught by the searchlight,' she warned. 'You must hide every time. It comes every seven to ten minutes.'

Here was yet another hazard for us to avoid. I wondered how we would cope during our swim. Anna said nothing.

Elsa led us back to the quay and pointed out some steps leading down to the water that lay several feet below us. Gerda whispered, 'You have to go now, while there is a break. Goodbye, and good luck.'

Our leave-taking was brief. Anna kicked off her shoes and I removed the boots I had been wearing, glad of the freedom from the discomfort of the last hour or so. I turned to her and whispered, 'Are you ready?'

She nodded and we picked our way carefully between the lumps of coal towards the steps. We glanced back to where Gerda and Elsa were watching us from the shelter of a building.

I climbed down the steps into what I expected to be fairly deep water, and received a shock. I was standing on mud, with just a few inches of water covering it. I helped Anna down, and we started out in the direction of the *Carl Lodeson*. We turned round and gave Gerda and Elsa a last wave.

We waded through the slimy mud, at times sinking deep into it, and I became fearful that it would suck us into its depths. We seemed to be making extremely slow progress towards our objective. Suddenly we saw the beam from the searchlight approaching again. There was nowhere to hide; all we could do was lie flat. After the light had passed over we emerged covered from head to foot in mud. I heard Anna whimper quietly, but there was nothing I could do to comfort her. We continued to wade out towards the ship, and all at once my feet gave way under me as I found myself entering deep water. It was time to swim for our lives.

Now that we were clear of the mud, our progress was faster. Ahead of us loomed the hull of the *Carl Lodeson*, looking dark and forbidding in the poor light. Anna demonstrated her superior swimming skills and reached the vessel before me. By the time I got to her, she was already pulling herself onto the rope ladder that hung from the side of the vessel. Captain Carlsen had kept his word – and we were not too late.

Anna carefully made her way up the ladder and the steep side of the ship. I followed slowly. As I made it onto the deck I looked back towards the shore. I guessed Gerda and Elsa had been watching to see our progress, but in the darkness it was impossible to make anything out.

Captain Carlsen emerged from the shadows, puffing on his smelly pipe. He nodded and lifted his hand by way of a greeting.

As we stood there miserably on the metal deck, with mud in our hair and dripping water, Captain Carlsen said, 'One moment,' and fetched a hose. It took us several seconds to realise what was going to happen, by which time we were being sprayed with water. Fortunately the pressure was fairly low. Suddenly Anna started to peel off the sodden boiler suit she was wearing. I watched in surprise as she discarded the garment and stood there in her underwear. Still, if it was good enough for Anna, it was good enough for me. I followed suit, remembering to salvage my passport and other possessions from the buttoned pockets.

The hosing-down ordeal could not have lasted more than a few minutes. The water was turned off and Captain Carlsen instructed us to follow him. He led us through a door into the interior of the ship and along a corridor. He threw open a door, turned on the light and motioned us to enter, accompanied with the words, 'You stay here until we sail.'

'When will that be?' I asked.

'Tomorrow morning.'

As it was now well after midnight, I assumed that he meant in a few hours' time.

We took stock of our new surroundings. We were in a small cabin, which looked as if it was not normally occupied and was used as a storeroom, because various bits of equipment

155

were scattered around on the floor and in a cupboard whose door was hanging off its hinges. The most welcome thing was that our two bundles of clothes, carefully wrapped up the previous evening by Elsa and Gerda, had been placed on a narrow bunk against one wall of the cabin. The immediate focus for both of us was the towels they had thoughtfully provided. Anna grabbed hers at once and commenced to dry herself. I followed her example and turned my gaze elsewhere as she slipped out of her underwear. Within a few minutes we were dry and a bit warmer, and we also felt a bit more respectable, each of us having donned a shirt that hid any embarrassment.

Anna glanced at her watch, which she had just replaced on her wrist. This prompted me to do likewise. The hands on mine showed that it was almost two o'clock. We eyed the bunk. Two minutes later we were lying side by side on the narrow mattress, covered by a rather tatty blanket. We were forced to be in extremely close contact, yet neither of us had the inclination to take things any further. We both quickly dropped off to sleep.

I awoke several hours later feeling a great need for a toilet. There was none in the cabin. I slipped off the bunk and quietly opened the door. There were several other doors opening off the narrow passageway. One of them had a vent, so I hoped that it might lead to what I was looking for. I carefully opened it. My assumption had been correct: in front of me was a rather dirty and smelly toilet.

Relieved, I made my way back to the cabin. Anna was sitting on the bunk, her feet dangling over the edge. The look on her face conveyed the question in her mind.

I smiled at her reassuringly. 'It's down the corridor,' I whispered. 'I'll show you.'

I led her to the toilet and then retreated to the cabin. Once there I attempted to have some sort of wash in the tiny basin. The flow of water was not good, but I managed to freshen up. I had not shaved for days and now had the beginnings of a beard.

Anna returned, making a face in the direction of the toilet. There was hardly any room for two people in the tiny cabin, so I lay on the bunk while she had a wash. She found a comb in her bundle, placed there by Gerda and Elsa, so she was able to give her hair some attention. I was a bit envious, wishing they had provided me with a razor.

It was still only a little after five o'clock. I wondered when we would actually sail and how long we would be confined for. Spending a lot of time in that tiny cabin without any natural light was not inviting.

'Do you think they will give us any food?' Anna asked.

'I hope so,' I answered. I had been wondering the same thing myself.

'I feel really hungry,' she declared.

'They can't let us starve to death.' I replied. I had used the term 'they' although so far Captain Carlsen was the only person we had seen on the ship.

We put on the rest of our clothes, including our underwear, which had dried out in the warmth of the cabin, and then returned to our former positions on the bunk to wait for something to happen. We were not there for long before there was a knock at the door. I sprang up to open it.

A blonde-haired woman stood on the threshold holding a tray. She smiled at us. 'Good morning,' she declared. 'I have breakfast for you.' She had a strong accent, which I figured out was perhaps Polish.

Anna sat up and we chorused, 'Good morning.'

The woman entered the cabin. There was no table, so she placed the tray on the bunk. As she turned to leave she smiled at us again. 'I am Karolina, Captain Carlsen's wife.'

'I am Tim, and this is Anna,' I replied.

157

Karolina nodded. 'I know.' She pointed to the tray. 'I come back for this in half an hour.' With that, she was gone.

Anna and I turned our attention to the food, which consisted of two generous bowls of cereal, toast with butter and some sort of preserve, and two huge mugs of coffee, black and strong.

We said very little while we concentrated on eating.

Half an hour later almost on the dot, Karolina returned to collect the tray. This time she had some news for us. 'We are getting ready to sail,' she announced.

As if to give substance to her words, almost at the same time there was a rumble, and a vibration shuddered through the ship. The engines had been started. Not long after that we felt a definite motion.

Anna now appeared to be more relaxed. 'I am so glad!' she exclaimed.

'It won't be long before we are away from the clutches of the DDR,' I remarked, sharing her feelings of relief.

However, the interlude of a more relaxed mood was short-lived.

Suddenly we heard shouting from somewhere up above us. We felt the motion of the ship stop and the engines fall silent. Within seconds the door of our cabin was flung open and Captain Carlsen stood there. He was clearly worried. He spoke immediately and without greeting us.

'The border control police are going to board the ship. They will search everywhere.'

Chapter 20

For a couple of seconds we must have appeared paralysed. Questions raced through my brain. Were we about to be discovered? Was Captain Carlsen going to hand us over to the police? Had this been the plan all along? Was Anna's fear of arrest going to be realised?

Captain Carlsen spoke again. There was urgency in his voice. 'Quickly. You must come with me.'

He turned and started to walk back along the passageway. Still trying to adjust to this new and alarming development, we slid down from the bunk, put on our shoes and hastened out of the cabin. Captain Carlsen turned to us abruptly and commanded, 'Take everything with you.'

Anna dived back into the cabin and grabbed our damp towels. As we followed Captain Carlsen through the narrow maze of passageways, I was almost certain that we were being led to our arrest. Anna's face told me that she feared the same thing. After all we had been through, it seemed that we had been lured into a trap. We came at last to the engine room, which was hot, oppressive and full of strange smells. There was the hiss of steam here and there. We walked past various pieces of machinery and eventually Captain Carlsen stopped before a metal door, which he opened to reveal a locker crammed full of cleaning materials, a mop and a broom, and buckets and paint cans littering the floor.

He quickly pulled these out of the locker. Next he lifted the whole floor to reveal a dark space beneath, as Anna and I watched in disbelief.

He produced a torch and flashed it into the dark space below. 'You have to hide in here.'

'Not down there,' Anna protested, alarm all over her face.

'You have to, or the police will find you. They will search the whole ship. This is the only place you will be safe. Hurry, please. They will be here very soon.' He handed me the torch.

It seemed that there was no alternative. I lowered myself into the space below and found myself in a cramped, tunnel-like area no more than four feet high. It was only possible to crouch or lie down in there. It smelt of oil and other unidentifiable disagreeable substances.

I did what I could to help Anna down, and as soon as we were both out of sight Captain Carlsen slammed the floor back into place. Above us we could hear the sound of the contents of the locker being replaced, followed by the closing of the door.

Anna lay down gingerly beside me. She gave an almost silent whimper and I placed my hand on her shoulder as a small degree of comfort. I switched off the torch to conserve the battery, and we were now in complete darkness. We were incarcerated and at the mercy of Captain Carlsen.

We were clearly right at the bottom of the ship. On one side we could make out the curve of the hull, and underneath the boards we were resting on we could hear water sloshing about. The smell was horrible, almost impossible to describe. At one stage I heard Anna lean over and retch. In the darkness, I found her hand and held it in mine in an attempt to give her some reassurance.

It seemed an age before anything happened, and then came the sound of loud voices and people moving about above us. The next instant we were aware of the sound of the locker door being opened, followed by the contents being moved about. I heard Anna whisper, 'Oh, no.'

We held our breath and waited for the trap door to be lifted, but after a minute or two we heard the locker door being slammed shut. We both breathed a sigh of relief. It looked as if our hiding place had gone undetected.

'They were so close,' Anna whispered.

'I know. We were seconds from being discovered,' I replied.

'I hope we will not have to stay in here for long,' remarked Anna. 'The smell makes me feel really sick.'

I agreed with her. The stench in our confined space was almost overpowering.

Now every second seemed like an hour. From time to time I would shine the torch on my watch, but the hands appeared to be barely moving.

Suddenly we heard the loud rumble of mechanical movement somewhere close by and we began to detect movement of the ship.

'I think we are underway again,' I whispered.

'Please, please let us out of this horrible place,' groaned Anna.

'They must do that soon,' I asserted, as much to comfort myself as to offer her some kind of reassurance.

Perhaps half an hour went by, and then to our relief we heard the locker door open and the cleaning equipment being moved aside. The next instant the floor was lifted and Captain Carlsen was smiling down at us.

'You can come out now,' he said.

We needed no urging. Anna was up at once and ready to scramble out, helped by Captain Carlsen. I quickly climbed up after her.

In silence we followed our host back to the cabin we had occupied previously. As he opened the door, Captain Carlson spoke again. 'You will have to stay in here until we dock in Denmark.'

'When will that be?' I asked.

'Before this evening.'

He closed the door and left us. I was relieved that we appeared to have escaped the scrutiny of the border patrol and best of all that Captain Carlsen had not betrayed us as we had feared he might.

I turned to Anna. 'You see? We made it. Captain Carlsen did not turn us in and we did not get arrested by the authorities.'

Anna nodded but did not reply. I was a bit puzzled and concerned by her next remark.

'I think I will lie down for a little while. I do not feel well.'

She lay down on the bunk, and I covered her with a blanket.

'Maybe it was the stench of that awful hole we were in,' I suggested. 'Try to sleep, then perhaps you will feel better.'

She nodded feebly as her eyes closed.

There was only one chair in the cabin, which I took possession of. Boredom was my main problem, as I sat there looking at the wall of the cabin and listening to occasional sounds coming from outside. I could tell by the stronger movement of the ship that we were now well out at sea.

I must have been sitting there for an hour or so when there was a knock at the door and I jumped up to see Karolina standing there with two mugs of cocoa. She placed them down on the chair and looked at Anna lying on the bunk.

'She's not feeling well,' I explained.

Karolina nodded. 'I get something for her.' With that she left us, returning a few minutes later with a glass of water and a small bottle of pills.

She bent over Anna. 'Take two of these. They will help you.'

Anna roused herself and obeyed Karolina, and then settled down again. She looked flushed, and tiny beads of sweat were on her forehead.

Karolina turned to me. 'If you wish, my husband says you can go up onto the deck for a while to get some fresh air.'

I thanked her and she immediately left us alone again.

I drank my cocoa, but Anna did not seem to want hers. 'I will drink it later,' was all she murmured.

After a short while I decided to accept Captain Carlsen's invitation. 'I'm going to have a bit of a walk on deck,' I said quietly.

Anna nodded, but said nothing.

I left the cabin and then realised that I had only a vague idea of how to find my way, although memories of our route the previous evening began to return as I walked along the passageway outside the cabin. A short flight of steps brought me out onto a small area of deck.

The morning was damp and grey. A kind of misty rain seemed to permeate everything, and visibility was almost zero. I was surrounded by grey sea, with no sign of the horizon. I turned my attention to the ship. I was surprised how small it was compared to my original impression. It seemed to be well past its sell-by date. Rust showed everywhere, and everything had an appearance of age and neglect.

I did not dally too long outside, as there was nobody about and nothing to see. On top of that it was cold. After a short while I returned to the cabin. Anna was still lying on the bunk, but she raised herself as I entered and looked at me enquiringly.

'It's not a very nice day,' I remarked. 'You didn't miss very much. How are you feeling now?' I could see that she still appeared flushed.

She gave a wry smile. 'I have a bit of a headache and a sore throat, but I think I'll be all right. The tablets Karolina gave me seem to have helped.'

'Good. I'm glad to hear that,' I replied. 'We should be approaching Denmark soon,' I added. 'I wonder where we will land.'

Anna took on an anxious look. 'I have no passport or documents. What will happen to me?'

'I'm sure it will be all right,' I replied, though I could see the problem.

There was a period of silence between us and Anna closed her eyes again. I resumed my position on the chair, picking up an old magazine that happened to be lying around and trying to read it. It appeared to be in Polish, a language I had absolutely no knowledge of. However, it was profusely illustrated, and the pictures were interesting to look at.

Perhaps an hour or so later Karolina arrived with some food. She seemed to be concerned about Anna and had brought some more medicine, a liquid that Anna told me afterwards tasted horrible.

After Karolina had left, we turned our attention to the food, which consisted of some kind of sausage and potatoes. I was hungry and quickly ate mine, but Anna merely picked at hers, though in the end I was glad to see that she did manage to eat a little. Afterwards she lay down again and closed her eyes.

Towards evening we heard the engine noise subside and more commotion going on above us. There was a gentle bump. Clearly the ship was docking. It must have been more than half an hour before there was a knock at the door. I threw the door open and Captain Carlsen stood there. He was full of smiles.

'We have arrived in Denmark,' he announced. He gave the name of the port we were in, but I was so relieved to hear the news that I missed it.

'That's excellent!' I exclaimed.

Captain Carlsen's next announcement was even more welcome. 'I take you ashore.'

On hearing the news, Anna immediately stirred to life, sat up and put on her shoes.

'When you are ready, I will show you the way,' said Captain Carlsen.

'Are you OK?' I asked Anna. She still looked as if she had a temperature.

She gave a hint of a smile, nodded and answered, 'Yes.'

I admired her determination, but I knew she was still not feeling at all well. I guessed the cold swim and hosing down of the previous evening had either aggravated an existing condition or started a new one.

We had very little to pack, and in two minutes we were ready to leave the confined space of the cabin.

The captain led us back up to the deck. A gangway now connected the ship and the shore. The dismal weather we had experienced at sea appeared to have cleared up and it was now quite a pleasant sunny evening.

I looked down at the quay. It was almost deserted, but I was alarmed to see two police cars parked there. Several policemen were standing around looking at the ship, evidently waiting for us to disembark.

Captain Carlsen made it quite clear that he was not going to accompany us off the ship. He stood next to the gangway and held out his hand, uttering a brief 'Goodbye, and good luck'.

Anna and I shook his hand and thanked him profusely. He received our appreciation with a smile and thanked us in return.

We looked up and saw Karolina standing on an upper deck giving us a friendly wave. Both Anna and I returned the gesture. Then she and the captain disappeared.

As we reached the bottom of the short gangway, two of the policemen moved forward to meet us. They greeted us with a friendly smile and the words 'Good evening'. Next, one of them asked us, 'May I see your passports, please?'

I quickly handed over mine. The policeman thumbed through it and asked, 'You are Timothy John Mallon?'

'Yes, that's me,' I replied.

The policeman nodded, thanked me and then turned his attention to Anna. 'May I see your passport?' he asked.

Anna shook her head. 'I have no passport,' she explained, looking miserable.

'Have you any other documents?'

She shook her head again and answered, 'No.'

His next question was 'Are you an East German citizen?'

'I am a citizen of West Germany,' Anna replied. 'I was kidnapped and held in the DDR. That is why I have no passport.'

'I can vouch for that statement,' I interrupted.

The policeman seemed puzzled. He looked at me, and then turned to Anna again. 'You will have to come with us and remain in custody while we sort things out.'

I saw at once a look of fear come into Anna's face. She uttered a hushed 'No'.

I rushed in. 'Look, we can explain everything. Just give us a chance.'

The policeman shook his head. 'I am sorry, sir, but we have our procedure to carry out for persons arriving from East Germany without documents.'

'But the lady is a West German citizen,' I protested.

The policeman remained unmoved. 'I understand that, sir, but she has arrived from East Germany without any identification.'

'At least give us the opportunity to explain,' I retorted.

'The lady will be given the opportunity to explain why she is here.'

I could see that we were getting nowhere. Anna remained silent, looking miserable and completely lost.

I tried another tack. 'The lady and I are living as man and wife. We should not be separated,' I pleaded.

The policeman remained unmoved. 'I am sorry, sir, but I have my orders to carry out. I am also instructed to provide security measures for you until you can be returned to England tomorrow.'

'What?' I exclaimed. 'On whose authority, and why do I need security protection?'

'I believe it is a result of a request made by your security authority in London,' the officer replied.

I was completely staggered by the suggestion. 'But you can't do that,' I pointed out. 'I am a British citizen, I hold a British passport, and I have committed no crime. I am entitled to freedom of movement.'

'I agree with you, sir, but I cannot disobey the instructions I have been given. It is for your own safety. Now, will you please accompany me?'

The policeman moved to usher me towards one of the cars. At the same time his colleague took hold of Anna's arm to escort her to the other one.

I could see that my cause was lost. I hoped that I would be able to sort things out later with somebody higher up the ladder. I watched helplessly as the policeman led Anna away. She glanced over her shoulder and gave me a look of desparation.

I tried to give her some form of reassurance and support. 'I'll see you later,' I called after her, confident that would be possible.

I suddenly thought of something else. 'The lady is not feeling well,' I pointed out to the policeman escorting me. 'She has a mild fever.'

'Do not worry. We will look after her,' he replied.

I watched as Anna was helped into the back seat of the car, and then, urged by the policeman who had done all the talking, I climbed into the rear of the other car, where a driver was waiting. My escort took his place in the front passenger seat and we were off, following the car that was carrying Anna.

I turned and looked back at the ship that had brought us to Denmark. The gangway had now been lifted up out of sight. I reflected that I did not even know the name of the town we had arrived at. Somehow it did not seem to matter. My concern was for Anna. Our parting had been abrupt and unexpected. I knew that, alone and ill, she must be feeling pretty awful as well as frightened about what might happen to her. My main hope now was to be able to talk to somebody in a more senior position and get things sorted out. In the meantime Anna and I were in the hands of other people and being taken to an unknown destination.

Chapter 21

The police car moved swiftly through the streets of the small town, which was basking in the last of the evening sun. I quickly lost sight of the car carrying Anna. Not long into our journey it turned off into a side road and disappeared. It was clear that I was not bound for the same place.

No conversation took place between the two policemen seated in front of me, and for the most part I was ignored. At one stage I asked them where they were taking me.

The policeman in the passenger seat turned to face me. 'We will take you somewhere to spend the night. Tomorrow morning we will take you to the airport and you will be put on a flight for London.'

'I see. Thank you,' I replied. It did not look as if I had any choice in the matter.

It was clear that I would not get any more information at present. I wondered where I was going to spend the night. Surely not in a police cell? I pondered the legality of holding somebody who had not been officially arrested. I was not kept in ignorance of our destination for long. After a short drive we turned off the road and parked in front of a large, imposing building. The number of police cars parked outside led me to conclude that it must be a police station. I wondered if my original concept of a night's lodging had been correct.

I was ushered out of the car and led into the building.

'Wait here, please.' One of my escorts pointed to a row of

seats facing a counter with several officers behind it.

I sat down and hardly had time to collect my thoughts before another policeman was standing in front of me, smiling. 'Good evening, Mr Mallon,' he said. 'Please follow me, and I will show you where you can sleep.'

I returned the greeting and stood up to comply. I was now convinced that I was going to be locked up for the night.

I followed the officer up a flight of stairs, along a corridor and then up a second flight of stairs to another corridor. The officer threw open a door and bade me enter. I walked past him into a small room. It contained a single bed, a desk and a chair, and an inner door that was standing wide open revealed a shower and a toilet. A window let in the last of the evening light. It was a light and airy room. I was relieved. At least I was not going to spend the night in a cell.

'This is one of the rooms used by our officers when they need to sleep in this building,' my escort explained.

'I see. Thank you.'

'Can I get you anything? Some food from the canteen?'

It was a welcome offer. It seemed ages since I had eaten anything.

'Perhaps a sandwich,' I suggested, 'and some tea.'

'I'll bring that for you,' the officer replied. He made to leave the room, but as he reached the door he turned and grinned. 'I will not be long. Don't go away,' was his parting remark.

I did not reply. I took the opportunity to look around my accommodation. It had all the basic requirements. I looked out of the window, but the view was only of a yard with parked cars.

A few minutes later there was a knock at the door. No one entered, so I moved over to the door and opened it. At least it had not been locked. An officer in uniform stood there. He appeared to be of a more senior rank than the policemen I had encountered previously. He held out his hand. 'Mr Mallon, I am sorry we have to detain you like this, but we have to carry out the orders we have received from London regarding your safety. I hope you will be comfortable here for the night.'

I shook hands with him and thanked him. Still baffled, I said, 'I am not aware of why I should need any form of protection.'

'We were informed yesterday that this would be necessary,' the officer replied.

The statement puzzled me even more. 'How did you know that Miss Bergmann and I would be arriving?' I asked.

'We were advised that you were coming,' he replied simply.

'Who instructed you to provide security arrangements?'

'Your security department in London.'

'But how did they know where I was?'

'I do not have that information.'

'So, what is going to happen now?'

'You will sleep here, and then early tomorrow morning we will put you on a plane for London.' The officer gave a slight smile. I wondered vaguely if the Danish police had been put on the spot.

'What is going to happen to Anna Bergmann?'

I was not expecting the answer I received.

'She will most likely be taken back to East Germany. My understanding is that there is a request from the East German authorities for her to be returned. They wish to ask her some questions.'

I was horrified and shocked by the statement. 'That cannot happen,' I protested. 'She is a citizen of West Germany and is about to become my wife.'

The officer was unmoved. 'We have no quarrel with East Germany. We may have to comply with their request.'

'That would not go down very well with either the West German government or Britain,' I pointed out.

My remark was greeted by a shrug. 'It is not a decision of the police department.'

Any reply from me was halted by the arrival of the officer carrying a tray of food. His superior took the opportunity to take his leave, I guessed with some relief.

'Enjoy your meal and have a good night's rest,' he said. With that he was gone.

The officer placed the tray on the desk. He smiled. 'Good night. I will see you in the morning.'

It was clear that as far as my hosts were concerned that was that. My concern for Anna had now become very acute. There did not appear to be anything I could do at present to help her. It seemed that the best approach would be to tackle the problem when I returned to London. I hoped she would not be transferred to East Germany immediately and that would give me time to work to have her released.

Seeing the food the officer had brought made me realise how hungry I was. I was impressed with what stood before me: two plates with several rounds of sandwiches containing a variety of fillings, and a pot of tea with milk and sugar.

I ate most of the food and then realised that it was getting late. I decided to turn in for the night and lay down on the bed, which proved to be very comfortable. At first I wondered whether I would be able to sleep after all that had happened, but I remained awake for no more than about ten minutes. Perhaps I was catching up after the previous nights of discomfort.

I awoke early and had already managed to have a shower before there was a knock at the door. I opened it to see the policeman from the previous evening.

'Good morning, Mr Mallon. I've brought you some tea. We have to leave for the airport at 7.30. I thought you might like this.' He smiled and held out a razor.

I thanked him and assured him it would be very useful. I now had several days' stubble on my face.

My thoughts turned to Anna again. 'I am not going anywhere until I know what is happening to my fiancée,' I said firmly.

At first the officer seemed taken aback, but he recovered quickly.

'I will try and find out some information about the lady,' he replied, and with that he left the room.

I sat and waited, quietly sipping my tea. Ten minutes later the policeman returned. 'I have made some enquiries,' he announced. 'It appears that the lady was taken to hospital yesterday evening with suspected pneumonia.'

My concern must have showed, because he hastened to try to reassure me. 'We will look after her, Mr Mallon. She is in good hands.'

I was still very worried, but I realised that there was not much I could do at this stage. After all, my logic went, as long as Anna was in hospital she could not be shipped back to the DDR. I nodded my agreement.

The policeman glanced at his watch. 'We will have to leave soon.'

I thanked him and assured him I would be ready. After all, I did not have much packing to do.

I took my time finishing the tea, sitting at the desk and watching the police officers coming and going in the yard below. When I had finished, I took the opportunity to have a quick shave.

At precisely 7.30 my host returned and advised me that it was time to leave.

I followed him down the stairs to the exit. A police car stood waiting outside, with two policemen already sitting in it. I was ushered into the back seat and we headed off for the airport.

My companions were mainly silent, though one jokingly enquired whether I had my passport with me. I assured him that I did.

We drove for what appeared to be quite a distance. It was almost an hour before the airport came into sight. I was quickly ushered into the terminal. Escorted by the two policemen towards a desk, I had never found checking in so quick and easy. Next came passport control, which was equally quick and trouble-free. Here my escorts left me after wishing me a good flight.

I made my way into the waiting area. I now had my boarding card, so I knew which flight was mine. I found a vacant seat and sat down.

I was surprised how quickly the passengers for my flight were called. My escorts had timed everything exceedingly well. With the rest of the passengers I made my way to the plane. It was not full and the other passengers appeared to be mainly businesspeople. No doubt many of them would be making a return flight in the evening. Such is the ease of modern travel.

Once we were airborne, breakfast was served. I was normally not a great fan of aircraft meals, but on this occasion I enjoyed the contents of the tray in front of me, including two cups of coffee. Having satisfied my hunger, I settled down for the rest of the flight. I was anxious to get home and start work on trying to help Anna. She was constantly in my thoughts and I wondered where she had spent the night and what she was going through. Over the weeks I had known her, I had steadily grown very fond of her. Now being separated from her was a big blow. I desperately wanted to be reunited with her. I determined that as soon as I was home I would contact Patrick. I knew he would have the right contacts, or would be able to point me in the right direction.

I must have dozed for a while in the warm atmosphere of the aircraft, for the next thing that I registered was the pilot announcing that we were approaching Heathrow and the instruction to fasten seat belts lighting up.

As I had no luggage, my passage through customs was quite quick. A swift passport check was the only formality. As I was emerging from the arrivals area I was surprised to see two policemen waiting there. They spotted me immediately and walked towards me.

One of them greeted me. 'Mr, Mallon, I am Police Constable Burgess, and this is Police Constable Edwards. We have instructions to escort you to your home.'

This was something I had not expected. 'That is very good of you,' I replied, 'but why all the attention?'

PC Burgess answered me. 'I am not aware of the details, sir, but apparently you require police protection.'

'I don't understand,' I replied.

'I am sure everything is in order,' he assured me. 'Have you no luggage?' he asked suddenly.

'No,' I replied, grinning. 'I travel light.'

My comment received a smile from both officers.

'Come with us. We'll get you home quickly,' said PC Edwards.

In a way these were welcome words. In the few days since I had left for Berlin a lot had happened, most of which I wished had not taken place.

I followed the two officers to where they had parked their car. A few minutes later we were speeding down the road, leaving Heathrow behind. The journey seemed remarkably short as the police car, in the expert hands of PC Burgess, weaved through the morning traffic. It was a pleasant sensation when we turned into the road where I lived.

'Which is your house?' I was asked.

I directed the officers to the gate. After a brief word of thanks from me, my escorts departed, mission completed.

I opened my front door, thankful that despite all my recent problems I had kept my key safely with me at all times. A sense of relief came over me. Several times during the last few days I had wondered when I would see my home again. I closed the door with its reassuring thump.

The first thing I noticed was the pile of mail Mrs Batty had placed neatly on the hall table. I promised myself that I would spend a leisurely hour later in the morning going through it all, but in the meantime there were far more pressing matters to deal with.

First I had a telephone call to make. Anna was still very much in my thoughts. I had to act quickly and try to retrieve her from Denmark before the police there had time to send her back to East Germany.

Chapter 22

I wandered into the kitchen, wondering vaguely whether I should make myself a mug of coffee. While I was debating, there was the distinct sound of the front door opening. It was Mrs Batty. She was immediately full of enthusiasm for my return.

'Oh, Mr Mallon, it's so good to see you. I was getting worried when you didn't come back when you said you would.'

I smiled at her. 'It's a long story,' I explained.

'Has Lena come back as well?' she asked.

'Not at the moment. Perhaps later.' I felt that at this stage I could not explain all the intricacies of the past few days, including Lena's change of name. Fortunately Mrs Batty did not enquire further.

She stood looking around, perhaps checking on my kitchen activities since her last visit. Her curiosity satisfied, she suddenly faced me. 'I bet you've not had any breakfast.'

'I've only just got back,' I replied, adding, 'I did have a snack on the plane.'

Mrs Batty tutted and shook her head. 'That won't do. Let me make you something to eat.'

'That would be nice,' I agreed. It seemed like ages since I had eaten a proper meal.

'Now you just sit yourself down.' Mrs Batty was already reaching for the pan. 'How about some scrambled eggs?'

'Fine,' I enthused.

In a very short time I was tucking into a hearty breakfast washed down with a mug of tea. While I ate, Mrs Batty chatted away about this and that, occasionally asking me something about Lena or my trip to Germany. I answered most of her questions with sufficient information to satisfy her, without going into too many details. I was anxious to get down to phoning Patrick as soon as possible. I knew that I probably didn't have much time before Anna was shipped back to East Germany. I had no idea how long she would be in hospital, but it was clear to me that as soon as she was well enough to be discharged no time would be lost before action would be taken regarding her future.

Suddenly Mrs Batty became flustered. 'Oh, Mr Mallon, I almost forgot to tell you. Yesterday a man called to see you. He said you knew him and he wanted to see you most urgently.'

'Did he tell you his name?'

Mrs Batty was clearly stumped for a moment. 'Now, what did he say it was…?' She was silent for a few seconds, desperately trying to remember. Suddenly it came to her. 'Yes – I remember now. It was Basil, or Boris, or something like that.'

'Boris Smirnov?'

'Yes, that was it.' Mrs Batty was clearly pleased that she had eventually remembered with a bit of prompting from me. 'Such a nice man he was.'

Evidently Boris had turned on the charm. Mrs Batty's revelation worried me slightly. After the unpleasantness of my last encounter with him, I wondered why he was contacting me again. I made a mental note to telephone him in due course, but Patrick must come first.

Mrs Batty suddenly thought of something else. 'Oh, he did ask me if I knew where you were and I told him you'd gone to Germany.' She looked anxiously at me. 'I hope it was all right to tell him where you were…'

I smiled at her. 'Of course it was,' I assured her, though I wished she had not done so. I did not trust Boris at all.

She nodded in clearly relieved acceptance of my reassurance and trotted off contentedly to do her vacuum cleaning. I finished my breakfast and was about to wash the dishes when she suddenly reappeared and reprimanded me. I found myself ushered from the kitchen, much to my satisfaction.

I hurried to my den and was just picking up the phone ready to call Patrick when the doorbell rang. I called out to Mrs Batty that I would answer it and hurried to the front door. Before I reached it, the bell rang again. Somebody was impatient.

I opened the door and to my surprise Pippa was standing there. Her sports car was parked on the drive.

'Surprise, surprise! I was in the area and thought I'd drop in to see you.'

I realised that this was the first time Pippa had ever called on me unannounced. I felt I had to invite her in, even though it was not a convenient time for me. 'Fine. Come in.'

I opened the door wide, stood back with a welcoming gesture and accompanied her into the lounge. She immediately plonked herself down into an armchair.

I was about to ask her what she was doing in the area, but she spoke first. 'Any coffee going?' Pippa did not mess about with fineries.

I grinned at her. 'Sure. No milk and one spoonful of sugar?' I queried as I rose to meet the demand.

'That's it,' Pippa replied, looking around at the contents of the room.

I went in search of Mrs Batty, who was happy to oblige and told me she would bring the coffee in when it was ready. I returned to the lounge. Pippa was now leaning back in the armchair, showing more of her legs than was perhaps advisable. It was unusual to see her in a skirt. She normally wore slacks.

I sat down opposite her and informed her that the coffee was in hand. I wanted to satisfy my curiosity. 'So, what brings you into this area?' I asked.

Pippa sighed. 'Oh, I had to see my solicitor. That's why I am dressed in this gear.' She looked down at her clothes. She suddenly added, 'And these damn shoes.' She glanced at the heels she was wearing, and the next instant she kicked them off.

I grinned at her. That was Pippa, direct to the point, no messing about. I was still interested in what she had been up to. 'Problems?' I asked.

Pippa made a face. 'Problem with my previous other half getting a bit stroppy. Have to sort things out.'

I was about to enquire whether the 'other half' Pippa referred to was male or female, remembering her preference in the past, but at that moment Mrs Batty entered with a tray containing two mugs of coffee and a plate of biscuits. She set it down on a nearby table, and I thanked her as she retreated.

The enquiring look on Pippa's face was plain to see. 'Where's Lena?' she asked.

'She's in Denmark.' My reply was intended to sound casual.

I handed Pippa a mug and offered her the plate of biscuits. As I did so she gave me another of her looks. She took a sip of her coffee, bit into a biscuit and studied me as she spoke.

'What's she doing in Denmark?'

Before I could reply she urged me, 'Come on, tell me. What's happened? I can see you're hiding something.'

I struggled with myself for a few seconds. I really did not want to go into the details with Pippa, and I needed to make that telephone call, but she was looking at me intently, so I knew that I was going to have to tell her what had happened. I just hoped that afterwards I would be able to get hold of Patrick.

As briefly as I could, I went over the events of the past few days. Pippa listened, sipping her coffee and consuming several biscuits. I ended up by explaining that I had had to leave Anna in Denmark.

As I concluded my story, Pippa put her mug down on the table and grinned at me. 'Another fine mess you've got yourself into.'

I did not share her analysis. She must have seen my reaction, because she immediately apologised when I did not reply.

'Look, I'm sorry. You know me. I'm completely on your side.'

I nodded. 'Thanks,' I replied.

Pippa was now quite serious. 'So, what happens now?'

I pondered the question for a few seconds before answering. 'As I said, apparently she's in hospital, but it's on the cards that as soon as she comes out she'll be taken back to East Germany. Apparently the authorities there have requested that she be returned to them.'

'How did they know she was there?'

'I've wondered that as well,' I replied.

'Why do they want her back in East Germany? I thought you said she was from West Germany.'

'Yes, but that doesn't appear to count.'

Pippa did not respond immediately. Then she asked, 'Can they do that?'

I shrugged my shoulders. 'It seems that in these circumstances they can.'

'What will happen to her in East Germany?'

'She will most likely spend a few years in prison.'

'Phew.' Pippa was clearly taken aback by my reply. 'I can see the problem,' she added quietly.

There was a short silence between us. Pippa was clearly absorbing what I had said, and I was going over events again and again in my mind, aware at the same time that I needed to contact Patrick. Every minute of delay could be critical.

It was Pippa who broke the silence. She spoke quietly again. 'You're very fond of this girl, aren't you?'

I nodded. 'Yes, I am. I just want her back with me.'

We talked for a while longer, and then Pippa said she had to go. I saw her to the front door and received her usual peck on the cheek.

As she was leaving the house, she turned to me and regarded me for a second. 'Remember Tim, I'm on your side. If there's anything I can do, let me know.'

'Thanks. I appreciate that.'

Suddenly I remembered something else. I called out to Pippa as she was getting into her car. 'Pippa, the clothes you lent Lena. They're all ready for you to take back. Shall I get them?'

Pippa shook her head. 'No. I'm running late now. Next time.'

I held up my hand to acknowledge her suggestion.

The next second, the car engine burst into life, and with a wave of her hand Pippa was reversing off the drive.

I gave her a parting wave, watched her go and went back indoors. Mrs Batty was just about to leave. It was much later than her normal departure time. I thanked her again and after a few courteous words she was on her way, remarking that she would pop in tomorrow to see if there was anything for her to do.

Two minutes later I was in my den and at last dialling the number I had for Patrick. I waited a long time before anybody answered. This time it was a man on the other end of the telephone.

I made my request to speak to Patrick Jenson. There was a pause, and then, 'Please give me your name.'

I immediately complied with the request.

'Do you have a security word?'

I repeated the code word I had given Patrick. I was then asked a number of further questions – where did I live, what was the nature of my business, why did I want to speak to Patrick, and so on. The interrogation must have lasted three or four minutes.

After all those questions, I was not prepared for what came next.

'Patrick Jenson is not available at present.'

'Can I leave a message for him?' I asked.

'Yes. I can take a message.'

I simply stated my name again and requested that Patrick get in touch with me. I stressed that the matter was urgent.

My request was duly noted and I was advised that Patrick would be made aware of it.

I put the phone down and felt completely shattered. I had not expected to be unable to speak to Patrick. I just hoped that he would respond to my request quickly. Every hour lost moved Anna's transportation back to East Germany closer.

The day was now well advanced. I pottered about here and there, sorting out the mail that had accumulated during my absence and looking over the pile of work that had collected on my desk. All the time I was on the alert for Patrick to call me back.

I was in the kitchen making myself a snack when the telephone rang. I hurried to answer it, my expectations high.

However, it was not Patrick.

'Tim, how are you, dear? We haven't heard from you for some time. We were getting worried.' It was my mother.

I suddenly realised that it was true that I had not been in touch with my parents for a while. Recent events had been absorbing so much of my time and thoughts that my long-promised visit to Bristol had not taken place.

I did my best to make a suitable apology. 'I'm sorry, Mum. I did mean to get down to see you several weeks ago, but something got in the way.'

'You sound worried. Is there anything wrong, dear?'

I could hear that my mother was getting anxious unnecessarily. I endeavoured to smooth things over. 'No, Mum. Really, everything's OK. It's just that I've had rather a lot on my plate the last few weeks. Hopefully, things will get better in the next few days.'

From her next comment, I could tell that she did not completely accept my explanation. 'You sound mysterious.'

I laughed, trying to allay her concern. 'Not really, but I must tell you that I've been to Germany since we last spoke.'

My strategy was appearing to work. My mother began to sound more relaxed. 'Germany? That's interesting. What did you go there for?'

'It's a long story. I'll tell you all about it next time I come over.'

'When will that be? It seems ages since we saw you.'

'I know. Just give me a few more days to sort things out, and then I'll come down for a weekend. Promise.'

Suddenly I had an idea. 'Perhaps Cherry and Roger could make it as well. It's been a while since we had a family get-together.'

My mother immediately took up the suggestion, as I knew she would. 'Oh, that would be nice. Cherry was asking about you the other day.'

Cherry was my sister. She was a teacher and she lived in Edinburgh. She was six years older than me and as a result we had never been really close. Since her university days we had tended to grow apart, particularly when she married Roger and moved to Scotland. Still, I concluded, a family gathering would be something to look forward to. If Anna had been there, it would have been nice to take her along and introduce her to my family. Somehow that idea now seemed very remote.

I put that thought aside and continued my theme. 'Sound Cherry out and see how they're fixed in the next few weeks,' I suggested.

'That's a good idea. I expect it would have to be a weekend, because of their work.'

'See what she says.'

'Yes, I'll do that, dear.'

I could hear some sort of conversation in the background, and then my mother was back on the line. 'Your dad wants to have a quick word.'

The next instant I heard my father's voice. 'Hello, old chap. What's new? I gather you've been to Germany.'

'Yes. Just for a few days.'

'Must be a story in that.'

'There is a story in it. I'll tell you all about it when I see you.'

I chatted to my parents for a little while longer. While it was nice to talk to them, all the time I was conscious that Patrick might call me from his home.

Eventually the conversation ended and I was able to put the phone down. It was now close to 8 o'clock.

For the rest of the evening I waited in vain. Patrick did not ring. I wondered how Anna was, what she was thinking, and where she was now. I knew that as time passed, her situation would become more critical and her deportation to East Germany closer.

Chapter 23

I woke up early the next morning after a welcome night's sleep in my own comfortable bed. By half past six I was down in the kitchen drinking a mug of tea and tucking into a bowl of muesli. Several thoughts occupied my mind. Uppermost was concern about how Anna was and what had happened to her. Not having any contact with anybody to find out more was a difficult and frustrating situation to deal with. It made speaking with Patrick all the more important. It also meant that I would have to stick around all day until he telephoned me. With that in mind I decided to go out early and stock up on food. My cupboard was now sadly depleted.

There was a supermarket no more than five minutes' walk away and I was searching its shelves within a few minutes of it opening. In the end I bought more than I needed and returned home laden with three bags. After sorting out all my purchases I went into my den. My work had been neglected rather badly in the last week or so, but at present I had little inclination to start on anything. Instead I paid several bills that needed dealing with and replied to a couple of letters.

I had been at it for just over an hour when the telephone rang. I answered it immediately, almost sure that it must be Patrick. Sadly, my hopes were dashed. When I had started writing full-time, I had quickly realised that writing novels, unless one hit the big time, would only produce a limited income, so I had taken on some freelance work as a technical writer, something I had previous experience of. The telephone call was from a company I had a current contract with, and it tied me up for nearly half an hour. While this work was my bread and butter, at the same time I kept thinking that Patrick might be trying to contact me.

Eventually the call ended. As I put the phone down I heard the front door opening. It was Mrs Batty. While I had originally only employed her services as a cleaner for two days a week, for a few hours each day, over the time that she had been coming to me her interest in me and my house had gradually increased and now very often she was there almost every weekday. In a way I quite enjoyed seeing her: at least I never got lonely. Though she only lived a couple of doors away from me, I guessed that, with two complaining teenage daughters and a husband who spent most of his spare time in the garden or watching television, her life was a bit dull and her visits to my house gave her a bit of stimulation and alternative interest.

I came out of my den just as she was closing the front door. She had a bundle of freshly laundered bedding under her arm. 'Good morning, Mr Mallon. I'll change your bed today,' was her greeting.

Mrs Batty had taken it on herself to do my washing as well as a hundred other jobs, so I usually paid her more each week than the original amount we had agreed on.

'Good morning, Mrs Batty,' I replied, as I headed towards the kitchen. Over my shoulder I called out, 'I'm going to make myself a coffee. Will you join me?'

'I will, but let me make it.' She was already hard on my heels.

I entered the kitchen one second in front of her. Once there, she passed me and made straight for the kettle. I smiled to myself. When I had issued the invitation, I had known what would happen.

Within a few minutes two mugs of steaming coffee had been produced. I sat down at one end of the table, and Mrs Batty sat at the other. It was unusual for us to have a drink together, but on this occasion Mrs Batty had a lot of things to relate to me and get off her chest.

I sat quietly listening while she told me that her husband, Bob, had won a hundred pounds on the football pools, and her elder daughter, Estelle, had suddenly given up her job in the supermarket and decided that she wanted to go into hairdressing. The problem it seemed was that Estelle had left the job before securing a new position. Mrs Batty had a strong opinion about her daughter's behaviour. Mostly I said nothing, just adding a comment here or there as appropriate. I guessed she welcomed the opportunity to talk to somebody outside her family.

We finished our coffee and then disappeared in the direction of our elected tasks. Mrs Batty headed to my bedroom, clutching the bed linen, while I returned to my den. I had hardly sat down when the telephone on the desk rang. Hurriedly I picked it up. I answered with my usual 'Tim Mallon.'

'Patrick here. You left a message for me. Sorry I couldn't get back to you yesterday.'

'Patrick! Thanks for ringing back.'

'No problem. First of all, how was Germany? You appear to have got stuck in the east.'

'Yes, I did. It's rather a long story.'

I heard a chuckle at the other end of the telephone. 'I already know some of it.'

This took me by surprise and I wondered how much Patrick knew. The channels of the security service seemed to be working very efficiently.

'That's what I want to talk to you about,' I began.

'You mean about Anna?'

Again I was surprised. How did he know it was Anna and not Lena who had been with me? This thought prompted my next question. 'How much do you know?'

There was a pause. 'Quite a lot. But how do you think I can help you?'

I had my question ready. 'I was told that Anna would be sent back to East Germany. That cannot be the case. She is a West German citizen. How can we ensure that she is returned to West Germany – or, better still, the UK?

'She's still in hospital,' Patrick remarked. It seemed that he was in possession of up-to-date information. This made me all the more determined to press my point.

'Yes, but what will happen to her when she is discharged?' I asked.

Patrick took his time to answer. 'Hmmm… That's a difficult one. Since she's not a British citizen, there's a limit to what we can do. It's really down to the West German authorities to intervene.'

'Can nothing be done?' I insisted.

'Not at this stage.'

I felt exasperated. 'But if it's left like that, the next thing is she'll be back in East Germany.'

'You're really concerned about her, aren't you?'

'Of course I am. I want to marry Anna.'

'Ah. I can see now where you're coming from.'

'So, what can be done?' I was determined to keep the pressure up.

There was silence at the other end of the line. I waited. It seemed ages before Patrick replied.

'Look, there's a lot going on about all this at the moment. Most of it is top secret. However, I can assure you that the matter will not be dropped. Leave everything with me and I will contact you as soon as I have some more information I can give you.'

Patrick's comment confirmed to me that there was more to the situation than I had imagined. I was also now quite convinced from his guarded remarks that he knew a great deal more than he was able to tell me. Unfortunately, that did not help my current situation, which was one of complete helplessness.

'OK,' I replied in a resigned tone. 'I'll just have to wait until you're able to tell me more.'

I was not expecting what came next.

'By the way,' Patrick asked, 'have you seen anything of Boris Smirnov recently?'

'Not for a few weeks, though he did try to contact me while I was in Germany.'

'What did he want?'

'I don't know. Why do you ask?'

'Just curious.'

I sensed Patrick was not being quite honest with me. The request that followed revealed that.

'If he does contact you again, let me know.'

My patience finally ran out. I was getting tired of information being withheld from me. 'Look, what's this all about? All this secrecy? And why was I rushed out of Denmark? You seem to know a damn sight more about all this than you are prepared to tell me. I feel I'm being used and kept in the dark.'

'Sorry if it seems to you to come over in that way. All will be revealed in due course. As to getting you out of Denmark, we thought that in the circumstances it was necessary.'

I was quick to reply, a surge of irritation sweeping over me. 'I was not aware that I was a security risk, or that I required police protection,' I retorted.

'Sorry if that's how it appeared.'

It was clear that I would get nothing more out of Patrick at this stage. I brought the call to an end. 'Well, thank you for contacting me. You know my position now. I would appreciate any further information about Anna as soon as you are able to tell me.'

'Will do. Goodbye for now.'

With a curt 'Goodbye' I put the phone down.

I was beginning to wonder what I had got myself into. My main concern was for Anna. Patrick appeared to know a great deal about what had happened in the last few days, yet at the same time he was not prepared to come clean about everything.

I felt I was being sidelined, an unimportant part of the game – whatever that was.

As I pondered my conversation with Patrick, Mrs Batty called out to let me know that she was leaving. I hurried out of my den to find her standing by the front door holding it slightly open, seemingly waiting for a few seconds to establish whether there would be any response from me.

I said goodbye and thanked her for her visit.

I returned to my den, intent on trying to clear some of the items that had built up during my absence. Just as I was about to start, I suddenly remembered the things I had left in the hotel in Berlin. On top of that I owed the hotel some money. I would have to make a telephone call and try to explain things. I was lucky that the woman who answered the phone spoke perfect English. I did my best to talk myself out of a difficult situation. Fortunately she was quite understanding, particularly when I offered to pay my bill in full. She advised me that they had kept all my belongings and asked me what I wished the hotel to do with them. There was nothing of great value among the items, but I felt I would miss the weekend case I had taken with me, as it was something I found useful. In the end we agreed that I would pay the carriage, and the hotel would send the items to me.

Having solved what had at first seemed a difficult problem, and feeling relieved that it had been settled amicably, I turned my attention again to trying to clear some of the backlog on my desk. I worked solidly for the next few hours, stopping only to make myself a mug of coffee, and at the end of that time I was pleased with my achievements. By the time I had finished, evening was fast approaching. My stomach was now reminding me that I had not eaten since my early breakfast. I went into the kitchen and made myself something to eat.

Anna was now constantly in my thoughts. I had been saddened and frustrated by the response I had received from

Patrick and I wondered if and when he would contact me as he had promised.

I had finished eating and was just starting on the washing up, accompanied with a mug of tea, when the telephone rang. I rushed to answer it, full of expectation. It was a surprise to hear my mother's voice again.

'Hello, dear,' she began. 'I hope I haven't interrupted anything.'

'No, Mum. I've just finished my evening meal. I was only doing the washing up.'

'Oh, good. I wanted to talk to you about the family get-together. I've had a word with Cherry and the only weekend she and Roger can make is the one after next. Will that be all right for you?'

I had a quick think. The weekend in question was a bank holiday one. Not the best time to be on the road, but there was no reason I couldn't go by train. At the same time Anna came yet again into my thoughts. It would have been nice for her to go with me. Now that idea was barely a faint hope. I returned my attention to my mother's proposal and made a decision.

'Yes, I could make that. It's a bank holiday weekend, though. The traffic on the roads will be bad. I shall most likely come by train. Let the train take the strain,' I quipped.

'Oh! Cherry and Roger will be driving down.' The surprise in my mother's comment reflected the fact that she was not a driver. For me, the thought of driving from Scotland to Bristol on a bank holiday weekend was definitely not appealing.

'Rather them than me,' I chipped in.

We continued to talk about various things, my mother clearly delighted that a family event was in the offing and already planning such things as a meal out for everybody and perhaps even a visit to the theatre. By the time we finished chatting, almost an hour had passed.

I returned to the kitchen and my washing-up and cold tea. I had just finished the dishes and was about to put the kettle on to make myself another mug of tea when the telephone rang again.

As I went to answer it, I wondered whether it was my mother again, with something else that had suddenly occurred to her that she wanted to talk to me about.

I was wrong. It was not my mother. It was Boris Smirnov.

Chapter 24

This was a telephone call I had not anticipated. After my last conversation with Boris Smirnov soon after Anna had arrived on my doorstep half-naked, barefoot and cold, and in the light of her subsequent disclosure of his treatment of her, I did not feel particularly well disposed towards him. However, there was no point in bringing up old issues. Nevertheless, my response to his call was guarded and certainly cool.

He appeared to be on good form. 'How's my old friend Tim?'

'Fine,' I replied.

'How did the German trip go?'

'It could have been better.' I wondered how much Boris knew beyond what Mrs Batty had told him, which had not been a great deal.

His next statement answered that question. 'So you had to leave Lena – or should we call her Anna now? – in Denmark.'

'Yes, I did.' It was now clearly emerging that Boris knew what had taken place. 'When did you find out she was Anna, not Lena?' I asked.

'Only recently, but I suspected something towards the end of her time with me.'

'You could have said something.'

'I wasn't sure, old boy. Anyway, I didn't want to spoil your pleasure.'

A tremor of irritation swept through me. I was silent for a few seconds.

Boris spoke again. 'When did you find out about her – ahem – dual role? In Germany, I suppose.'

'That's correct.'

'Fooled me and fooled you, the little bitch. Well, she'll get her full deserts where she's going.'

'What do you mean?' Boris's remark alarmed me, though I could already guess what he was referring to.

'Hasn't anybody told you? She's going to be sent back to East Germany. The East Germans have made a formal request for her return. A few years in an East German prison will tame her down a bit.' He chuckled. 'Who knows? She might even end up in a Russian gulag. That would sort her out. Serve her right.'

I could not comprehend Boris's attitude and his callous remarks about Anna, and I was certainly not going to join in with his condemnation of her. 'But Anna is a West German citizen and she has done nothing to the East Germans,' I pointed out.

Boris laughed again. 'Fat lot of good that'll do her. Even her American friends won't be able to get her out of the predicament she's in now. The Stasi'll make sure of that.'

Boris was beginning to irritate me intensely. I felt sure that his vicious condemnation of Anna was unfair and uncalled-for. 'You seem pretty sure of that,' I replied.

'Inside information, old boy. Sorry – can't divulge my sources.'

'I see,' I retorted icily.

'So,' continued Boris, 'what did you do in East Germany besides getting stuck there?'

'Not a lot,' I replied.

'But you met Max Meyer.'

Boris certainly appeared to know a lot about my recent activities. I resolved to say as little as possible in reply. 'Yes, I did.'

'What did he want you for?'

'He wanted to know where Lena was.'

'Did you tell him?'

'Yes, I did.'

'Did he mention me?'

'No. All he was interested in was Lena.'

I was getting fed up with Boris's interrogation of me. 'You're asking me a lot of questions,' I protested before he could quiz me again.

'Sorry, old boy. No offence intended. You know me.'

I was about to reply, but he continued. 'Anyway, I wanted to ask you a couple of other questions.'

'If you must.'

My coldness did not deter him. 'What did you find out about Lena?'

'That she was dead.'

'I see.'

I was sure Boris was already aware of this, but he wasn't going to let me know that. My reply was sharp. 'I don't know what you see. You most likely know a great deal more than I do.'

'Could be. But I was interested to hear what you'd discovered in East Germany.'

'Well, I've told you most of it,' I retorted. I was beginning to tire of the conversation.

Perhaps Boris sensed that, because he suddenly changed tack. 'Why don't you come over to my place again sometime? You can meet Olga.'

'Who's Olga?'

'She's the current woman in my life. She's Russian. She's fantastic. Tall, blonde, lovely legs, gorgeous figure. You'd like her.'

Vaguely I wondered if he was trying to get rid of Olga in the same way he had offloaded Anna on me. 'How long has she been with you?' I asked.

'Only a couple of weeks.'

I was about to respond, but Boris repeated his invitation. 'Look. Let's fix a date. When can you come over?'

At that stage, after everything that had happened, spending time with Boris was the last thing I wanted to do. 'Weekends are the best time for me, and for the next couple of weeks I have something else on,' I replied.

'After that, then.' He was certainly being insistent.

'OK. I'll keep it in mind.'

'Splendid. I'll look forward to it. Don't forget.'

It was Boris who ended the call. 'I'm afraid I've got to go now, old boy. Got to get back to something called work.'

'I know the feeling,' I retorted.

'Talk to you again soon. Cheerio for now.'

'Goodbye,' I replied, relieved that the conversation was over. The line went dead.

I replaced the handset. Boris's comments about Anna being sent to East Germany troubled me deeply. Clearly he must have access to some inside information. If what he had intimated was true, it did not bode at all well for Anna, but all I could do was wait until Patrick got in touch with me again. I trusted him more than Boris and I decided that I would give more credence to what he would have to say.

The evening was now well advanced and I decided to turn in for the night. Unsurprisingly, sleep would not come. I tossed and turned while the hours ticked away. All the time my thoughts were on Anna. Where was she? What was happening to her? I knew she had a horror of East German prisons, after her previous experience in one. The big question was when I would see her again – if ever.

It was the early hours of the morning before I finally fell asleep, and as a result I did not wake up at my usual early time. Even so, I stayed for a while in bed contemplating the events of the previous day.

Eventually I got up and after a quick shower and a shave I went downstairs to the kitchen. By this time the newspaper had arrived. I collected it on the way and indulged in a rare event, reading it while having some breakfast. I had almost finished eating when the telephone rang. Glancing at the clock,

I suddenly realised how late it was. I had a sudden feeling that it might be Patrick phoning. I picked up the telephone, gave my usual greeting and waited, expecting to hear his voice.

It was Pippa.

'So you're up.' Such was her greeting.

'Of course,' I replied, adding, 'I'm surprised you're up so early.'

'Don't be like that, or I won't tell you the news I've got for you.'

I chuckled. 'That sounds interesting.'

Pippa was in one of her teasing moods. 'It is interesting, but before I tell you I want to know what the payment is going to be.'

I laughed out loud. I knew what she was after. However, I decided to play along with her game. 'That depends on what the news is,' I replied.

'It's about Anna.'

I came down with a bump. How did Pippa have information about Anna? All she knew so far was what I had told her. Intrigued, I composed my response. 'OK. If it's good news, I'll stand you another meal out.'

'That will be two you owe me.'

'Point taken, but what's the news?'

Pippa adopted a more serious tone. 'Right. Enough of this frivolity. Down to business.'

My patience was beginning to ebb. 'I'm waiting,' I replied.

'Well…' Pippa spoke slowly, clearly choosing her words carefully. 'The thing is that she is now out of hospital.'

'That's certainly good news. I'm curious to know how you found out.'

'There's more to it than that.'

A horrible thought came to me. Was Pippa about to confirm that Anna was being returned to East Germany? I was impatient to know, yet at the same time I dreaded the answer.

'What?' I asked.

I had the feeling that Pippa was enjoying relating her news. She was certainly taking her time responding to my prompting.

Before she could speak again, I butted in. 'Please tell me what's happened.' My anxiety was creeping into my voice.

Pippa continued her slow delivery. 'Well, I have it on good authority that arrangements are being made for Anna to travel back to West Germany.'

The news struck me like a thunderbolt. This was a bit of a contrast to what Boris had told me. I had to know more. 'What? Are you sure? How did you get this information?'

I heard Pippa chuckle. 'Well, it so happens that my partner's work means he has important contacts in Denmark. It's a case of who you know.'

'So it's accurate?' I queried.

'Absolutely.'

'Gosh! That's a bit different...' I was thinking aloud.

'What do you mean?' Pippa retorted.

'Sorry. I was just thinking. Boris Smirnov rang me yesterday and he told me Anna was being sent back to East Germany.'

'Why did he say that?'

'I have no idea. He must have had a reason.'

'Well, believe who you will. I've done my best.'

I could hear that Pippa was a bit put out by my comment. I rushed to smooth things over. 'I'm sorry. I didn't mean to sound ungrateful. If it comes from the horse's mouth, your version must be the correct one.'

'Of course it is.'

'Well, thank you very much for letting me know. Thank your partner as well.'

'Will do. And don't forget, you owe me two meals now. I worked jolly hard to get that information.'

'In what way?' I asked.

'Persuading a certain person to obtain it.'

'Well, you were certainly successful.'

'Yes. But I had to resort to extreme measures.'

I was about to reply, but she continued. 'I had to threaten no sex until he got the information.'

I burst out laughing. 'You didn't!' I exclaimed.

'I jolly well did! And you see, it worked.'

'You're a shocker, Pippa.'

'I know. Born that way.' She was getting quite flippant.

'Well, you'd better bring him along when we go out for that meal,' I suggested.

Pippa did not seem very enthusiastic. 'I might,' she replied casually.

I wondered whether this was the partner she was having problems with. No doubt I would find out in due course.

Pippa interrupted my thoughts. The tone of her voice was again quite serious. 'Tim, just one thing. My partner broke every rule in the book to get this information. Keep it to yourself. He could get the sack if it leaked out.'

'Of course,' I replied.

'Anyway,' Pippa continued, 'now that Anna is going to be in West Germany, what will you do?'

I thought for a second. This was something I had not contemplated, so I had given no thought to my next move. 'I'm not sure at this stage. Wait a day or two, I think.'

'Sounds a good idea. Let me know what happens.'

'I will – and thanks again for all your efforts.'

'No problem. I must go now. I thought I'd give you the news before I went out.'

'That's really thoughtful of you. Thank you.'

'OK. Keep me informed. Cheerio for now.'

'Cheerio,' I echoed, as she put down the phone.

I stayed at my desk and tried to do some work, but my concentration was not good, so my output was limited, Anna being constantly in my thoughts. The rest of the day passed slowly. Mrs Batty made her usual visit and spent some time giving me an update on her family's activities. Of course, she asked me if I had heard from Lena, which made me think of Anna again.

I kept thinking about Pippa's telephone call and how it contradicted Boris's assertion. I prayed that her version was the correct one, but that did not stop me from wondering why Boris had been in possession of a completely different story. I waited impatiently to hear what Patrick had to say. In view of the changing situation, I thought I might hear from him quickly, but it did not happen. Frustrated with waiting, several times I almost rang him but at the last minute changed my mind.

It would be three days before he called me.

Chapter 25

I had just finished what for me was a late breakfast when the telephone rang. As I rushed to my den to answer it, I glanced at my watch. It was just before nine. I wondered who could be contacting me so early.

It was with a feeling of surprise that I heard the voice at the other end.

'Good morning, Tim. Patrick here.'

'Good morning,' I echoed. I could not help adding, 'Gosh, you're early.'

I heard him chuckle. 'Yes. I had to come into the office to sort out a few things.'

I could not wait any longer for information. 'What news have you got for me?' I asked.

There was a pause before he answered, and when he did I could tell from the tone of his voice that what he was about to tell me would not be welcome. 'There has been a new development, but not what you were hoping for.'

'Tell me,' I urged. After my conversation with Boris, I was now fearing the worst.

'Anna has been sent back to East Germany.'

Even though I had half expected to hear this, the news struck me like a thunderbolt. For a few seconds I was too shocked to reply.

Patrick must have realised this, because he spoke again. 'I'm sorry. I know you would have wanted a different outcome.'

'What will happen to her now?' I asked.

Patrick was non-committal. 'Who knows? At best she will probably get a couple of years in prison.'

'Can nothing be done? What about the West German authorities? Can't they intervene?'

'Oh, they will go through the usual formality of demanding her return, but it won't make any difference to what the East German state wants to do. Don't forget there is considerable tension between the two countries.'

'What will she be accused of?' I asked glumly.

Patrick obviously thought about my question for a few seconds, because there was a delay before he replied. 'It's hard to say. I'm sure the East Germans will come up with something. They might even accuse her of spying.'

'But it was her sister Lena who did that,' I protested.

'You don't have to be involved in anything to be accused of something in a place like East Germany. You must realise that you were under scrutiny just for trying to contact Lena. You were lucky you were helped in time before you could be picked up. '

My head was in a whirl. Patrick clearly knew a great deal about my movements. How did he find out? Who was his informant? He and Boris Smirnov were the only two people I had spoken to since I got back to England.

I probed Patrick for more information. 'How do you know so much about my time in Berlin?' I asked.

He chuckled again. 'I'll let you know one day.'

It was quite clear that Patrick had no intention of divulging any more information to me. I was annoyed by his flippant reply. I had apparently been a key player in something or other, but the details were not going to be revealed to me.

'I see,' I replied, a little curtly.

It was at that point that I suddenly remembered my telephone conversation with Boris Smirnov. 'Oh, by the way,' I said casually, 'you wanted to know if Boris Smirnov had been in touch with me.'

'Has he?'

'Yes. He phoned me a few days ago.'

'What did he want?' Patrick's reply was quite sharp.

I thought for a few seconds. 'He wanted to know what had happened to me in East Germany,' I explained.

'Did he ask about Lena?'

'Yes, he did,' I replied. 'I told him Lena was dead.'

Patrick did not respond to this revelation. Instead he asked another question. 'Did he mention Max Meyer?'

'Yes. He asked me if Max Meyer had spoken to me about him.'

'What did you say?'

'I told him he hadn't.'

'I see. Thank you.'

Patrick's string of questions did not make sense to me. Clearly my answers were meaningful to him, but it all seemed to be a bit of jumble to me. Once again it came over loud and clear that there was a great deal more to everything than I was going to be told.

'Well, I hope it all makes sense to you,' I remarked. 'I'm afraid it's a complete mystery to me.'

Patrick laughed briefly. 'Sorry about that.' He brought our conversation to a close. 'Look, I'm sorry, but I'll have to go now. I have an important meeting in ten minutes. I'll let you know of any further developments.'

'Thank you.'

'OK. Goodbye for now.'

I hardly had time to reply before he put the phone down.

I slowly replaced my own telephone. I remained sitting in my chair. The news Patrick had conveyed to me was slowly sinking in. So Boris had been correct. Anna had been sent back to East Germany. There still remained the information I had received from Pippa, but now, with this latest announcement from Patrick, it seemed that might be false. Boris and Patrick had told me the same story and somehow I felt that their version must be the correct one. My hopes of a happy outcome had been dashed. I wondered where Anna was now and how she was coping. I guessed she must be feeling pretty awful. Wild thoughts came into my head. Would I be able to contact her? Would I be able to send her a letter? It was all too vague, with too many unknowns. On top of everything, the injustice was hard to comprehend. Anna was being victimised simply because she was Lena's sister. Now it seemed probable that she would receive no help from anybody and would just be abandoned to her fate. I felt defeated and helpless. All I could do was wait and see what the future would bring.

For the next few days I waited anxiously for news of Anna, but none came. I tried to settle down to some work, but I was always on the alert for a telephone call, and disappointed when the calls that I did receive were not what I was hoping for. I was even reluctant to leave the house to go shopping for food, just in case someone phoned while I was out.

Mrs Batty came and went, on several occasions asking me if I had any news about Lena. I could not bring myself to explain in detail to her what was happening. Instead, I just answered that Lena was unable to return at present. To date, I had not even told Mrs Batty that the person she knew as Lena was in fact called Anna. Somehow, at the present time, it seemed unimportant.

As the days passed, I grew more and more despondent and anxious. In desperation, on several occasions I telephoned Patrick's office, but I was unable to speak to him. I left my name and asked for a return call, but he did not contact me.

As the time slipped by, I came to the conclusion that either he had no information or he was unwilling to contact me and preferred to let matters rest. Perhaps Anna was no longer of any interest to his mysterious department. She had served her purpose and could now be dumped.

The family gathering my mother had arranged came up quite quickly. I managed to book a seat on the train and travelled to Bristol on the Saturday. My sister and her husband were already there when I arrived. After that it was round after round of chat, catching up on each other's news. It was a pleasant weekend, even if it was a little bit exhausting.

It was not until I was alone with my parents that I went into detail about my visit to Germany. They were quite sympathetic to my plight, but of course there was little they could do other than make the right noises. I did not think my mother quite understood the difference between East and West Germany, but that did not really matter. Of course, talking about things brought Anna yet again into my thoughts.

Before I left, my mother took me on one side, clearly anxious to say something to me. 'Don't forget,' she stressed, 'your father and I want to meet Anna as soon as possible.'

I assured her that they would do so one day, but even as I spoke the words, doubt and uncertainty clouded over me. Would that ever happen? And if so, when?

I returned to London on the Tuesday. Back home the gloom that had been present before my weekend away returned. It was now getting on for two weeks since my last conversation with Patrick. I no longer had the heart to ring his office. There did not seem to be any point. Instead I threw myself into my work, staying in my den from early in the morning until late in the evening. While this self-imposed therapy did not stop me thinking about Anna, at least I was keeping myself busy and relatively productive.

I had been back home for several days when I awoke to a bright sunny morning. The sight of the sunlight coming into my bedroom tempted me to depart from my current routine. Instead of my usual early breakfast, I decided to take a walk and replenish my stock of food. I knew it was too early for the supermarket to be open, so I killed some time with a walk around the nearby park. Even so, I still had to wait a few minutes outside the store before the doors were opened. It was the best part of an hour later that I arrived home laden with bags. As I opened the front door, I heard the telephone ringing. Dumping the bags and slamming the door behind me, I made a grab for the hall telephone, wondering who could be calling me so early.

I hardly had time to answer before Patrick's voice came over loud and clear. 'Good morning, Tim. I thought you were out.'

'I was,' I replied, adding a hurried greeting.

'Tim, I need to see you urgently.'

'I've been trying to contact you,' I replied. My tone was perhaps a little critical.

'Yes, I know. I'm sorry I was unable to get back to you.'

Patrick's reply irritated me. I had been leaving message after message, never receiving a reply, and now all I received was a casual apology with no explanation. Now he wanted to see me urgently. I waited for the next move to come from him.

'I do want to see you,' he stressed.

'Any particular reason? Do you have some news about Anna?'

'Yes, I do. There have been more developments since we last spoke. That's why I need to see you.'

The mention of Anna made me forget my irritation with Patrick. 'Can't you tell me over the telephone?' I asked.

'No. It's better that I see you in person.'

I could sense that he was not going to budge. 'When?' I asked.

'Today. This morning. Can you make it?'

I could now sense the urgency in his voice. Something drastic must have happened. Whatever it was, I wanted to know about it quickly. Briefly I considered Patrick's suggestion. I had no commitments. My decision was quick. 'Yes, I can. What time?'

'I'll send a car for you. Can you be ready for ten?'

I glanced at my watch. That would give me less than an hour, and I still had not had any breakfast, but I could fit everything in.

'That would be all right,' I replied, adding as an afterthought, 'but I can come on the train.'

Patrick was insistent. 'No. I'm sending a car.'

I gracefully accepted the offer. 'OK. Ten this morning it is.'

'Right. See you later.'

With that he was gone.

I put the phone down, picked up my shopping and hurried into the kitchen, breakfast being my first priority. It did not take long to produce a bowl of muesli and a mug of tea. All the time I was puzzled by Patrick's call. Why did I have to go to London? Why all the secrecy? For several days I had been trying to get hold of him without success, and now out of the blue he had contacted me and everything was suddenly urgent. It was odd, but now I was keen to see him as soon as possible. I was anxious to learn what information he had about Anna. I was pleased the appointment was for that morning and I would not have to wait any longer for news.

Chapter 26

I had changed my clothes and was ready by the time the clock on the wall showed the hands coming up to ten. A large black car drew up outside my house. A young man in full chauffeur's uniform got out, walked up to my front door and rang the bell. I hurried to open the door.

'Mr Mallon?' he asked.

'Yes, that's me,' I replied.

'Good morning, sir,' he said. 'I am instructed to drive you to London.'

I replied as cheerfully as I could, grabbed my trusty rucksack and locked the door behind me. The young man escorted me to the car. I would have preferred to ride in the front beside him, but he was already holding the rear door open for me.

The journey was made mostly in silence. Attempts on my part to start a conversation did not meet with any degree of success. In the end I accepted that talking was not on the cards and sat back and took in the passing scenery.

Once we were in London, progress was much slower. I noted the route we were taking, crossing the Thames on Waterloo Bridge and then driving into the South Bank area. Eventually we pulled up outside a small office block.

The driver turned to me. 'If you would like to go into reception, sir, they will direct you.'

I thanked him, alighted from the car and entered the building. I could see no indication anywhere of who or what occupied the building. A middle-aged woman was sitting behind a desk in the small reception area, flanked by two security officers who scrutinised me as I approached.

I gave the woman at the desk my name and told her the reason for my visit. There was a delay while details were checked, and then I was asked for my password. Eventually, when everything appeared to be in order, I was instructed to proceed to the fifth floor, where Patrick would meet me.

I made my way to the nearby lift, closely observed by the two security officers. I was glad when the door to the lift closed and I was out of their gaze. Stepping out of the lift on the fifth floor, I found myself in a long corridor, which must have run the length of the building. It was lined with doors, but they were all closed. I wondered how I was supposed to find Patrick. I need not have worried: as I walked along the corridor, looking at the names on each of the doors, suddenly a door opened ahead of me and Patrick appeared.

He greeted me cheerfully. 'Tim, thanks for making it. Come in.'

I followed him into a light, airy office with a plush carpet on the floor, dominated by a large desk and several chairs.

Patrick closed the door behind us. He turned to me and grinned. 'Do sit down. Would you like some coffee?'

'That would be nice,' I said.

I sat down on one of the chairs facing the desk. Patrick had turned his attention to the coffee percolator that stood on a side table. After a minute or two he placed a cup on the desk in front of me, commenting, 'No milk, no sugar,' as he did so.

'That's fine,' I replied, taking a sip of the dark liquid.

Patrick poured himself a cup and then took a seat opposite me. 'You must have been wondering what was happening when you didn't hear from me,' he began, looking at me with a hint of a smile.

'I have to say that I did,' I replied, somewhat coldly. The

memory of the last few days of waiting and receiving no answer to my telephone calls was still uppermost in my mind.

Patrick looked at me for an instant and then leaned over the table towards me. 'Look, I completely understand how you must be feeling. I would feel the same way myself. The truth is that a lot has happened since we last spoke and events were moving at a fast pace. It was impossible to involve you in things at that stage and keep you informed.' He continued to regard me after he had finished speaking.

I gave a nod and a non-committal 'I see' by way of a reply.

I was anxious to learn why I had been brought to London. More than that, though, I wanted to know what had happened to Anna. I steered the conversation towards that subject. 'You indicated that you had some new information about Anna.'

Patrick smiled. 'Yes, I have, but there has been another important development.'

'What?'

Patrick studied me intently, as if to ensure that he had my undivided attention. 'Boris Smirnov and his partner have been arrested.'

'What? How?' This news out of the blue quite stunned me. I tried to formulate a more coherent question. 'On what charge?' I enquired, my head reeling.

Patrick settled back into his chair. He appeared to be completely calm and composed as he replied. 'They will face charges of espionage. Boris Smirnov has been under surveillance for some time.'

I tried to take in the information I had just been given. It almost seemed to be unbelievable. 'But... But I thought he had quite an important job in the security service,' I managed to get out.

Patrick smiled briefly. 'He did. That's the problem.' He took a sip of his coffee, carefully replacing the cup on his desk before continuing. 'Once all this reaches the press, it will be headline news. There will be a few red faces in high places. It's even possible some heads will roll.'

I drew in a sharp breath. 'Gosh. That's quite incredible.'

Patrick nodded. 'Yes, it is. Max Meyer has also been arrested by the West Germans. It's all been a huge operation that has been going on in the background for months and months. Security information was being leaked to Russian agents and it was necessary to find out who was involved.'

I was silent for a few seconds, trying to piece together everything I had just heard. A lot had been happening of which I had been completely oblivious.

I voiced my thoughts to Patrick. 'I seem to have got myself involved in something major, except that I've been piggy in the middle.'

Patrick responded with a laugh. 'That's a good way of putting it,' he replied, still smiling.

'Well, I can tell you that I most certainly did not relish the role,' I replied. I still felt a bit sore about the way I had been treated, and I was desperate to know what had happened to Anna.

Patrick leaned across the desk again. 'Look, Tim, I know all this has been tough on you and you've been kept in the dark about things, but the truth is that we didn't know how much you were involved with Boris Smirnov.'

'I see,' I replied. 'What about now? And, more to the point, where is Anna?'

Patrick grinned at me. 'You wouldn't be here listening to all this if we had any doubts about you.' He paused for a second before continuing. 'We felt concerned when you went to Germany, but when you started looking for Lena Bergman our fears diminished.'

I was puzzled by his last remark. 'You mean you knew that Lena was actually Anna right from the start?' I asked.

'Absolutely. It was all part of the greater plan that she should assume the part of Lena while she was here, and—'

'Including with me,' I interrupted.

'Yes, I'm afraid so.'

I thought for a moment, remembering what Anna had said to me at the farmhouse. 'Anna told me she was recruited in West Berlin to attach herself to Boris and pretend to be her sister.'

'That's right,' Patrick replied. 'We needed somebody to keep an eye on what Boris was up to. We relied on his attraction to women to help things along. Unfortunately, things didn't work out quite as well as we had hoped.'

'You mean, because he got tired of her and dumped her on me?'

Patrick smiled at me. 'Exactly.'

'But where is she now? And what about what happened to us in East Berlin?' I asked.

Patrick had a ready answer to my second question. 'Your meeting with Max Meyer put you in a dangerous situation. We had to move fast to get you out of the country before you were picked up by the East Germans.'

I drew a deep breath. 'Phew. All this was going on, and I was an innocent player.'

Patrick nodded.

While it was interesting to hear from Patrick the background to everything that had taken place, I was still desperate to know what had happened to Anna. 'You still haven't answered my question about Anna. Where is she?' I demanded.

Patrick gave me a bit of a grin before he replied, 'She's safe and well.'

'I don't understand. Where is she?' I could sense that he had some good news.

Patrick was serious again. 'She spent a few days in hospital recovering from influenza before going back to Germany.'

'What part of Germany?' I asked, fearing his reply.

Patrick had a twinkle in his eye as he replied. 'West Berlin.'

His statement took me by surprise. After everything I had heard, this was the last thing I expected. 'But you told me a few days ago that she was being taken back to East Germany,' I protested. As an afterthought and to add weight to my statement, I added, 'Boris Smirnov told me the same thing.' In order to protect Pippa, I did not mention the contradictory information she had given me.

I immediately received a nod of confirmation from Patrick. 'That's correct. That's the story we circulated, because it was necessary at the time. It was all part of the plan. In fact, the East Germans never asked for Anna to be returned to them at all, and the Danes played their part admirably.'

I said nothing. So Pippa had been correct and I had been fooled by both Patrick and Boris. I felt rather put out that I had been taken in in this way, particularly in view of my part in the whole business.

Patrick must have sensed my reaction, because he immediately tried to appease me. He leaned across the desk again. 'Look. I know we misled you, and in the circumstances it was a pretty rotten thing to do. But in this business you sometimes have to do some rotten things and take actions you'd rather not take.'

He looked at me, waiting for me to reply.

I took my time answering. Looking at things logically, it didn't really matter what had been said. The essential thing was that my fear that Anna would end up in East Germany had come to nought. It was time to put aside my pride. 'I understand,' I said simply.

Patrick nodded agreement. 'Good.'

I could have thought of more things to ask him, but I was stopped short by his next question.

'Are you happy with what I've told you about Anna?'

I pondered the question for a few seconds. For me the important thing was that Anna was safe in West Berlin and not languishing in some East German prison wondering what was going to happen to her. I had already made up my mind that I would contact her as soon as I could, even if it meant returning to Berlin. 'I think so,' I replied.

Patrick glanced at his watch. 'Good. Then in that case I'll have to kick you out soon. Got another of those damn meetings coming up before lunch.'

It was clearly time for me to leave. I started to get up from my seat.

Patrick reacted immediately. With a wave of his hand he instructed me otherwise. 'No. Sit down. I want to introduce you to somebody before you go.'

'Who?' I queried. I could not think of anybody else in Patrick's domain who might want to be introduced to me, or, for that matter, who would be of any interest to me.

Patrick was clearly not going to enlighten me. 'You'll see in a moment,' he replied with a grin.

He leaned towards the intercom on his desk and spoke into it. 'Ready for you now.'

Several minutes passed, while Patrick and I engaged in trivial conversation.

Suddenly there was a gentle knock at the door and then it opened. At first I did not recognise the fair-haired young woman who entered. She was dressed in a pristine white blouse and a tailored skirt, and she carried a matching jacket over her arm. Her hair was piled up in a practical fashion. She could have just stepped out of a top-level business meeting.

As she closed the door and walked towards us, confident in the high heels she was wearing, recognition dawned and one word escaped from me. 'Anna.'

Her face lit up on seeing me, and she exclaimed, 'Tim! What are you doing here?'

Patrick stood up and grinned at me. 'Tim, meet our most reluctant agent.'

'I guess I already know her,' I replied light-heartedly.

Patrick waved Anna to a chair. 'Let me get you some coffee,' he offered.

'I'd love some,' she replied. 'I got up in the middle of the night to catch the first plane here.' As Patrick busied himself with the coffee percolator, she sat down, adjusting the tight skirt over her legs. Her eyes were on me, questioning.

'You came from Berlin this morning?' I asked her.

She smiled. 'Yes. And I'm here legally this time.'

Patrick handed her a cup of coffee and took over the conversation, smiling broadly and addressing me. 'We summoned her here to thank her for her good work – and,' he added chuckling, 'to sack her.'

'I didn't do very much,' Anna responded thoughtfully. She gave a little laugh. 'But I don't mind being sacked.'

'The part you played was very important,' Patrick interjected. Then, suddenly solemn, he addressed her again. 'I'm very sorry about what happened to your sister.'

Anna's expression turned to one of sadness. 'Thank you,' she whispered. I placed my hand on hers. She looked up and gave me a hint of a smile.

Patrick waited a minute or so before speaking again. 'Anyway,' he said to Anna, 'I have no doubt you will be pleased to hear that you are now formally released from your commitments with this department.'

'Thank you,' she replied.

'You know what's happened to Boris Smirnov?' Patrick asked her.

Anna nodded. After a pause, she asked, 'What about Max Meyer?'

'He's been arrested by the West German authorities.'

'He is not a nice man.'

'I agree with you,' said Patrick. 'Some of the things he's done make it difficult to have any sympathy for him.' He continued thoughtfully. 'He has been playing a double game for years. Even the East Germans were getting a bit suspicious of him. He has been losing favour with them for some time and it seems they were as concerned about him as we were.' He hesitated and then looked straight at Anna. 'Kidnapping you in London was one last desperate attempt on his part to regain some favour with the East Germans. I hope your ordeal was not too bad.'

Anna was silent for a few seconds and then remarked, 'It is best forgotten.'

After a few more minutes of conversation she suddenly looked at her watch and glanced at Patrick. 'I have to go very soon. My plane back to Berlin leaves at three o'clock.'

Her remark prompted Patrick to look at his own watch. 'Heavens!' he exclaimed. 'I've got an important meeting coming up in fifteen minutes.'

It was a clear sign that the meeting was over. We all stood up and Anna and I prepared to leave. I drained the last of my coffee. There was the usual shaking of hands and words of thanks and then Patrick showed us to the door of his office.

As we made our way along the corridor to the lift, Anna glanced at her watch again. I knew what she was thinking. She didn't have much time before her flight.

Once we were in the lift I put my arm round her. In high heels she was as tall as me. 'Do you really want to catch that plane?' I asked, smiling at her.

She looked at me, enquiringly. The next instant she snuggled into my shoulder. 'Can I come home with you?' she whispered.

'That's my hope,' I replied.

Suddenly we were in each other's arms, kissing passionately.

We walked out of the building hand in hand.

 Matador